Table of Contents

The Marquess of Secrets
The Hornsby Brothers #3

By
Karyn Gerrard

The Hornsby Brothers Series

THE SONS OF THE DUKE of Gransford are diverse in their natures, as are their choices when it comes to love. Each man is determined to hold out for true love since they grew up in a loving household. Searching for it, however, is different from finding and leads each of the Hornsby brothers to unlikely places and chance encounters with what society would consider unsuitable women.

BOOK #1 *is Bold Seduction (Of Professor Hornsby)* and concerns the youngest son, Spencer Hornsby.

Book #2 is *The Vicar's Frozen Heart* and concerns the middle son, Tremain Hornsby.

Book #3 and the trilogy's conclusion is *The Marquess of Secrets* and involves the oldest son and heir to the duke, Harrison Hornsby, the Marquess of Tennington.

I should have included an author's note with book one when it was released with a publisher and clarified about the youngest Hornsby brother, Spencer. I apologize for not including this, as some readers were confused by Spencer's actions. If diagnosed today, Spencer would fall on the spectrum of a mild form of autism. In the Victorian era, there were a few recorded accounts of children manifesting similar aspects. Back then, they were usually diagnosed with "children's psychosis" and admitted to the asylum.

Summary

A SECRET LIFE

Harrison Hornsby, Marquess of Tennington, heir to the Duke of Gransford, has been a scandalous rake for years. Unbeknownst to all, he'd been leading an entirely different and secret life as a physician to the poor. Though his younger brothers held out for true love, as the heir, Harrison feels he doesn't have that luxury. The time has come to marry an appropriate bride—one who, in society's eyes, is worthy of becoming a duchess. But fate has other plans.

A DAMAGED WOMAN

LIFE FOR LYDIA CHESTERTON has not been kind. Once a respected nurse at a London hospital, she is alone and homeless due to disastrous decisions concerning love and trust. Lydia lives on the streets and is deathly ill and finds temporary sanctuary with Harrison. Her rescuer is hard to resist, especially when he proposes a trade of secrets. With her dangerous past threatening her future and Harrison bound by duty, a lasting love appears out of reach—unless they toss aside all obstacles and risk their hearts.

Chapter 1

LONDON, APRIL 1882

Harrison Hornsby, the Marquess of Tennington and heir to the Duke of Gransford, lay on his mistress's bed—wholly spent. A thin sheen of sweat covered his body. The session was vigorous and bittersweet, for this would be the last time he'd visit Francesca Whitten, his paramour of three years.

Harrison believed he was growing too old for such doings, considering he turned thirty-four two weeks past. It was better to end this association before initiating his search in society's marriage mart.

His unspoken obligation was to find an appropriate bride amongst the aristocracy, a woman with the carriage and grace to one day become his duchess—and to be the mother to his children. Such a task was a centuries-old tradition and expected within the peerage. It was all well and good that his two younger brothers, Spencer and Tremain, married for love. He would not and could not allow himself such a luxury.

A firm believer in duty and all it entails, Harrison alone stood as the future of his family name and title, and his choice of bride was paramount. Harrison held out for as long as he could, hoping to fall in love like his brothers. Yearning for a love match his parents enjoyed was always a gamble and infrequent amongst the aristocracy.

Francesca interrupted his thoughts by arching her foot and trailing it along the back of his leg and across his buttocks.

"I've always admired your muscular and very firm arse, Tennington," she purred. "You're in fine fettle for a man who spends his time sitting in Parliament. It is where you spend your time, is it not? You come here so rarely; I've begun to fashion all sorts of scenarios."

Her foot caressed him, stirring his arousal. Surprisingly, he was ready to go again, but there will be no acting on it.

"Pray tell, what scenarios?" Harrison murmured, struggling to stay awake regardless of his physical reaction. He should be taking his leave, but this was the first time in weeks that he had time to relax in any way.

"At first, I thought it might be another woman. But you're not the sort of man to engage in sensual deceptions, even if I am your mistress. Then I thought you had a family secreted away in an isolated hamlet on the other side of the country. Again, it's not in your personality. Regardless of the scandal, you would acknowledge any bastards."

"Yes, I would."

"Not that you would be so careless in your dealings to even have illegitimate children. You plan things meticulously. I concluded that you are as eccentric as the rest of your family." Her foot halted in its exploration. "Oh, I am sorry."

That killed his arousal. Tossing the silk sheet across his naked body, he turned and sat upright.

Eccentric. Well.

He was wide awake now. "What have you heard?"

Gossip and societal machinations annoyed Harrison to no end. Yet, they were all around him as society thrived on chatter, whether the tittle-tattle had merit or not.

No one dared to speak about scandalous intrigues before the Hornsby family. Not while Harrison's father, the Duke of Gransford, remained one of the queen's favorites. And a powerful force at court and in the House of Lords.

Francesca had the grace to blush. The crimson color of her cheeks matched the reddish shade of her hair. "I don't wish to end this glorious afternoon with an argument," she stated, her lower lip thrust out.

"I give you my word that I will keep a tight rein on my annoyance. Please, do tell." He crossed his arms, watching her closely.

With a sigh, she met his gaze. "It is said that your youngest brother, Lord Spencer Hornsby, is—mad, suffers fits and inappropriate emotional outbursts. Because of it, he has hidden away in a remote Wales location not to embarrass his family."

The fury growing inside Harrison was potent, but he struggled to conceal it. However, there was no denying Spence was—different.

From earliest childhood, Harrison observed how Spence struggled with managing his emotions and other personality quirks.

Doctors were called in. All agreed that the boy must be carted off to an asylum. To the duke's credit, he would not brook any such suggestion. His father could be a force to reckon with when pushed too far. Protecting the family took priority, and Harrison respected his father for taking such a stance.

Observing Spence's travails firsthand sparked Harrison's interest in the study of medicine. He was a registered physician with the Royal College of Physicians, with degrees from Cambridge, but, alas, being a peer would not allow him to open a public practice. According to society, it was not an accepted role for the heir to a duke. One must adhere to the blasted rules. But he kept up with the latest developments in medicine.

Harrison encouraged Spence to place a rigid routine in his life to keep the demons at bay. Doing chores or tasks a certain way at the same time of day placated Spence and lessened the outbursts. Also, focusing on one study—like his research into the ancient Byzantine Empire—calmed him.

His brows furrowed. All Harrison ever wanted was to protect his youngest brother, but no matter what he'd done to try and divert the gossip, Spence was laughed at and talked about regardless.

"My youngest brother is not mad, contrary to malicious chatter. As a matter of fact, he's to be married in May."

Francesca bit her lower lip.

"What?" he asked, dreading the response.

"I've heard his fiancée is a prostitute. Not that I'm judging, God forbid."

How in blasted hell had that information seeped out? To say Spence's and Tremain's choices of brides were outside the norm of so-called proper society was an understatement. Not that Harrison cared about their backgrounds, but all the best to his brothers and their soon-to-be brides.

All the more reason that Harrison must ensure his choice was beyond reproach. It was best to deflect any further scrutiny into his family's personal business.

His parents were tolerant and progressive in their thinking and accepted both women warmly, but Harrison was well aware that the constant gossip hurt them, particularly his mother.

"I can trust you to keep this to yourself?" he ventured.

Francesca crossed her heart and nodded. "Absolutely. I'm known for my discretion. Though others do not hesitate to tell me things, I reveal nothing." She snuggled under the bedspread, and her eyes brightened with anticipation.

It was true; her tactfulness was one of the reasons he'd chosen her for his mistress.

"The week between Christmas and New Year, two of Spencer's friends hired a prostitute as a birthday gift. The madam herself took the assignment. Long story short, the week alone at a snowbound lodge in Wales resulted in a proposal. They are to be married next month."

Francesca smiled. "Falling in love in one week! How utterly romantic! Have you met her?"

He had, not two weeks past. The family gathered at Gransford Manor so he could meet not only Philomena McGrattan, the ex-madam, but Tremain's fiancée, Eliza Winston, the ex-governess.

Philomena's gentle guidance and empathetic nature calmed Spence, and he focused all his restless energy on her, and she reveled in it.

A good match in all ways.

Harrison had believed that Spence, for all his foibles, would never find someone to love and love him in return. How gratifying that he had.

"Yes. For all of Philomena's tragic back story, she is a lady of courage and compassion. I am well pleased for my brother."

She smiled warmly. "Then I'm glad. I don't like repeating this prattle, but I suppose you should be aware, as no one would dare say it to your face."

True enough.

"But you will?"

"Well, yes. I genuinely *like* you, Tennington. I cannot say as such with all the men that have been in my life." She cuddled close to him and ran her fingertip along his lower lip. "Though you come here far too infrequently, I enjoy it when you do."

"I did tell you to take on another if you wished," Harrison said.

"No, I don't juggle multiple men. Besides, the older I've become, the more I enjoy the solitude between your visits. And you're most generous. I have no complaints about renting this town house, the servants, the horse, the carriage, and extra money." She drew her hand away and gave him another brilliant smile. "Besides the energetic bed sport, I like that you stay and talk. Take a meal. Oh, do you wish for me to ring for food? I ordered a platter of sliced meats be available, along with assorted cheeses, fruit, and fresh bread."

Tempting, but Harrison was not staying long enough to partake of food. "Perhaps later. Pray continue with the Hornsby gossip. I am all attention."

"Are you certain?"

Hell, it must be bad.

"Yes. I have steeled myself for what comes."

"It is said that your middle brother, Tremain, perpetuated a scam for his own selfish needs. He pretended to be a country vicar for a nefarious purpose. Since his war injuries have rendered him impotent, he took in a street urchin as his son."

That, as they say, takes the cake. Unbelievable. Again, Harrison's blood boiled. He took a deep breath and exhaled, hoping to contain his exasperation.

"Tremain is a hero of the Anglo-Zulu War, and though his injuries were serious enough to require surgery, a lengthy recovery, and using a cane, as far as I'm aware, he is not impotent. He, too, will be married next month, the same day as Spence," he huffed in frustration.

"But his injuries were not only physical," Harrison continued. He was revealing too much, but he trusted Francesca. "I observed the despair Tremain had sunk to. He needed to heal, and, to his credit, he accomplished it his way. You see, he studied for the church and has a divinity degree. Instead of joining the church after graduation, he chose to join the army."

The tale riveted Francesca; it was plain on her face. Yes, he no doubt revealed too much, but he entrusted her with keeping her word.

"He wished to give something back to humanity, serve his fellowman in a way that did not involve war and killing," Harrison continued. "I admire him for it. The family gave him the distance and time he requested to achieve those goals. Not only did it help thaw his frozen heart, as he called it, but it allowed a serene peace to enter his life—and a new spirituality. It opened his heart to love."

"This bit of gossip on your viscount brother originated from Lady Samantha Trimly by the by," Francesca interjected. "Vindictive piece of baggage. Also claimed your brother seduced a member of his congregation, a haughty governess of questionable background. The tale claims the lady of the house dismissed her for seducing one of her sons. I take it she is the woman he's to marry."

"Yes, she is." Harrison rolled his eyes.

Good God above.

Tremain's gossip traveled far and wide thanks to Lady Trimly, no doubt jealousy the main reason.

Eliza, Tremain's fiancée, could be considered haughty at the first meeting as her mode of speech was formal. Harrison surmised it was her upbringing in the orphanage and instruction by the nuns. But he soon concluded that Eliza possessed a generous, warm nature. Perfect for his brother.

"I feel rather cross now that I've repeated this malicious tittle-tattle; it put me right out of sorts," Francesca pouted teasingly.

"Then this should cheer you up." Harrison reached for a wooden satin-covered box and handed it to her. "Buttercreams from H.I. Rowntree and Company. I know you like them. They have begun to carry a new confection developed in Switzerland: milk chocolate."

Francesca squealed with delight as she adored chocolate. After opening the box, she peeled away the parchment paper. "Is it this lighter color, the milk chocolate?' she asked, her eyes sparkling.

"It is. Try it. I found it far sweeter than the dark one."

With a contented sigh, she bit into the small candy. "Delicious. I like the extra sweetness. Thank you, Tennington. You are thoughtful."

"Lift the tray," he coaxed in a soft voice.

She gave him a puzzled look but did as he asked. Her hand flew to her mouth to cover her gasp of shock. "Are they emeralds?"

"Yes, they are. I know you adore gold bracelets. Those tiny stones are emeralds."

Pulling it over her wrist, she gave him a radiant smile. "This is exquisite. I love it. Thank you, Tennington. I daresay this is almost as if this were a dismissal gift." Francesca's smile deflated. "Oh, this is goodbye. I had a feeling this was coming."

"There is more."

Francesca lifted the folded papers from the sweet box. She quickly scanned them. "You're giving me this house and the contents?" she whispered.

"Yes. It's yours to do as you will. It is not a large residence as town houses go. Live in the place, sell, or use it for your next affair, whatever you wish." He took her hand and kissed it. "It is goodbye, along with a heartfelt thank you. You kept up the pretense I was an unrepentant rake, and I appreciate the effort."

"I was a handy excuse and glad to maintain the illusion you kept me busy every night when in fact, you were not." She gave him a sad smile. "I will confess I'd hoped you would come more often. I truly did."

Harrison had other commitments—ones he would not reveal to Francesca, regardless of the trust between them.

She tapped the papers thoughtfully against her chin. "There will be no one else after you, Tennington. It's time to retire. I may be older than you think."

"Indeed? Care to elaborate?"

"I turned forty-two, three months past."

By God, she didn't look it.

"You are remarkably well-preserved," Harrison teased good-naturedly.

"It takes great care and effort to maintain such a state. It's time for Francesca Whitten to fade into the mist and for Annie Stokes to step forward. I think I will purchase a seaside cottage in a small village. Perhaps I'll meet a tall, broad-shouldered, handsome vicar much like your brother. My vicar will be distinguished, with a touch of gray at his temples. And will not care a whit for my past."

Harrison laughed. "You are a treasure, Francesca, or should I say—Annie?"

"That's my real name. You're the only one I've ever told."

He kissed her forehead, pushed the sheet away, and stood, looking for his clothes. Once he located them, he began to dress.

"You are a man of many secrets—a true puzzle. But I respect that you keep your covert life to yourself," she whispered.

A covert life. If she only knew.

"Look at me, Harry."

It was the first time she'd ever used his first name. He halted doing the buttons on his waistcoat and turned to face her.

Her expression was determined but laced with concern.

"If any man deserves true love, it is you, my dear. My severance package indicates that you will be shopping for a young lady of the aristocracy to be your bride—such a cold and loveless arrangement. I don't see that for you, Harry. I feel you will follow your brothers down the path of true love with a woman, not of your class."

She gave him a sad smile. "She may even be entirely inappropriate. If you meet such a lady, do not dismiss her. Nor dismiss what you feel. True love is rare, and many never experience it. Promise me you will give it a chance."

"Quite a speech. I have obligations—"

"Are your parents insisting you make an aristocratic match?" she asked.

"No, not at all."

"Then do not force the issue. Look by all means, but do not settle for anything less than true love. I'm giving advice and perhaps overstepping my boundaries, but it is kindly meant. I wish for you to be happy. As I said, you deserve love, and all it offers."

He nodded, too moved to speak. Blast it all; he didn't think his parting from Francesca—Annie—would affect him this deeply.

Clearing his throat, he said, "May you find all you desire, Annie."

"And you as well, my dear."

Slipping on his greatcoat and donning his hat, he exited the room and trotted down the stairs. Stepping into the night, he thought about her emotionally spoken words.

"I feel you will follow your brothers down the path of true love with a woman, not of your class. She may even be entirely inappropriate. If you meet such a lady, do not dismiss her. Nor dismiss what you feel."

He was the heir with an unspoken duty to marry well; because of it, he couldn't afford the luxury of loving someone not of his class.

It would be prudent to remember it.

Chapter 2

A WEEK LATER
East End of London

Of all the wretched nights Lydia Chesterton had endured the past few weeks, tonight was the worst. She'd run out of money four days past and slept out of doors because of it.

Lydia spent the last night in a dingy alley, crammed behind empty beer casks. The entire area smelled of stale beer, urine, and mold.

Though she managed a few hours of rest, the temperature dropped during the night, and she'd caught a chill.

The truth? Lydia had been feeling poorly for more than a week.

She understood enough to be aware that she was dehydrated, malnourished, and well on her way to developing full-blown pneumonia. In her previous life—one that seemed to belong to someone else—she worked as a nurse at a well-respected hospital.

How far she had fallen.

But now was not the time to ruminate about her past and the many mistakes therein. Lydia needed immediate shelter and medical care.

Where could she possibly go?

The voluntary or charity hospitals turned away the genuinely destitute, which described her current condition. There was the option of a poor law infirmary, but she'd be forced into a workhouse once recovered.

A fate she wished to avoid.

Last night she overheard a conversation in the alley, two men speaking of an underground respite from life on the cobbles. The location was in an abandoned, partially dug underground railway line next to St. Dunstan's Church in Stepney.

More of an illegal soup kitchen, yet the Anglican nuns offered a pallet and a blanket, and a surgeon tended to the sick for no cost. The men referred to him as Doctor Damian.

It sounded too good to be true. Lydia clutched her pathetic bundle and calculated the distance she would have to walk. She could be there in less than an hour if she didn't collapse from exhaustion or sickness.

First, she must eat.

Lydia pulled the stale raisin bun from her wool coat pocket. She'd located it in a rubbish bin outside a tearoom. When one was starving, one could not be fussy. Because of rampant hunger, she ate it far too quickly, and her stomach roiled in response. But she had no choice but to push on.

Besides, what were the chances John Huntsford was even looking for her? Yet, the loathsome man was vindictive enough to hunt her down. There was nothing else for it; she must keep moving.

Wiping her runny nose with her tattered sleeve, she headed toward Stepney High Street.

At last, the medieval tower of the centuries-old church came into view, and she nearly cried in relief. Next to the old church was an archway made of brick, covered by large wooden doors with a sign declaring "Keep Out."

Did she come all this way for nothing?

Lydia's heart sank until she observed people entering and exiting by moving aside, then replacing a few loose boards.

Tentatively, she did the same. Numerous torches in holders lit the way. Lydia ambled along the tunnel a short distance, and it opened up in what would have been the platform area. Beyond the dais, they halted the work as there were no more bricks. The dirt walls shored up the crudely-made massive wood timbers. On the wood platform were six brick columns. The nuns kept their workstations in and around the columns.

Pallets filled every bit of the ground, and two wood stoves were throwing much heat with two large cauldrons sitting on top. In the dimly-lit tunnel were the dregs of society: lost, desolate, impoverished people with no one in the world or place to live.

The place was crowded. There were many castaways in whose number she could count herself. The sight saddened her.

Despite the workhouses and debtor prisons, many people lived on the streets when all else had failed them. Or, in her particular case, when horrible life choices brought one as low as one could possibly sink.

Shivering, Lydia had no idea where to go.

One of the Anglican nuns saw her swaying on her feet and rushed forward to take her arm. "I'm Sister Monica. Come, warm yourself by the stove."

Lydia wanted to cry but was so weak and weary she couldn't even summon the tears.

"Along with me, four other nuns working here trained under Florence Nightingale in the Crimea. So we know what we're about," Sister Monica continued. The nun, who looked to be in her early sixties, had a kindly face, her voice firm and soft with empathy. "Take a seat on this bench."

Still clasping her small bundle, Lydia moaned as waves of warmth rolled over her from the nearby stove, immediately chasing away the worst of the chill.

"I'm going to ask you a couple of questions. How long have you lived on the streets?" the nun asked.

"I-I ran out of money four days past. I've been sleeping in alleys."

"You don't look well at all. Are you what is considered an 'unfortunate woman?'"

It took Lydia's bewildered and weary mind several moments to work out what the nun meant.

No, she had not taken money for sex thus far. However, it may become her last resort. No wonder so many poor women—and men—turned to prostitution. Lydia vowed never to look down on anyone in such a circumstance again.

"Not as yet," she whispered.

"I ask to determine if you're suffering from disorders of the trade. I will fetch you a bowl of broth. First, I will explain the rules of this underground sanctuary. This terminus is temporary; you cannot stay here permanently. This is, literally, the end of the line. From here, the only option is the workhouse or, if deemed ill enough, one of the charity infirmaries. Or you can allow us to find you honest work for you to regain a footing in society."

Regain a footing in society.

Not likely, not after what she'd done.

Lydia nodded. At this point, she would agree to anything to stay sitting by the fire with a bowl of watery broth.

"Good. Doctor Damian will be along directly to see you. He'll decide how long you will remain here."

Damian.

She just caught on to the name now. "The patron saint of physicians?"

"Oh, are you Catholic?" Sister Monica asked.

"If I am, does that mean I cannot stay?"

"Nonsense," the nun huffed. "There are no denominations here. Only those in need."

"I'm not Catholic, but my mother was." But not a practicing one.

The nun gave her a sympathetic look. "Was? Past tense? Do you have any family to turn to?"

Lydia swallowed the lump in her throat and whispered, "I have no one. At all." She lowered her head in sadness and shame.

The nun tsked, patted her arm, and then bustled to the stove.

Lydia exhaled a shaky breath. The air down here was not the best. The odor of damp earth mingled with the redolence of humanity.

A child cried in the distance. But despite the wail, this somber place was eerily quiet.

What was there to be cheerful about?

There were people of all ages and, no doubt, from various backgrounds, including families with children and babies. Undoubtedly, they would be given top priority for assistance.

As they should be.

As a nurse, she'd observed the best and worst of humanity. What the nuns were doing here was the best, to be sure. It made her proud to be part of the profession.

Sister Monica returned and passed her a bowl of broth and a wooden spoon. Lydia was surprised to see a goodly amount of vegetables swimming about, along with small pieces of ham.

A true feast.

With tears in her eyes, Lydia profoundly thanked the nun. She nodded in reply, then moved off to attend to others.

Lydia returned her attention to the soup. It was her first hearty meal in days.

Slow and easy.

Though tempted to shovel the stew down her throat, she savored every spoonful. It warmed her insides and calmed the hunger spasms. When finished, she placed the bowl and spoon on the floor as exhaustion overcame her.

Using her bundle as a pillow, she curled up on the bench and drifted into a deep sleep.

"Miss?"

Lydia snapped awake, and her head turned toward the deep male voice. A man all in white stood before her.

She struggled to sit up, and he clasped her elbow gently to assist her. A jolt of heat moved through her at his brief touch.

Rubbing her eyes, she took a closer look. Tall and broad-shouldered, the man wore white shirt, coat, and trousers. A large apron adorned with small blood spatters covered most of the clothes. He wore strange white gloves, his face obscured by a white mask, and his hair hidden under a white cap. A stethoscope hung about his neck.

All she could see were large silver-gray eyes studying her closely.

This man must be Doctor Damian. Dressed all in white, he indeed resembled an angel of mercy.

"I'm a physician here to determine your state of health and how long you will remain here."

Quality.

Though the mask muffled his voice, he possessed the unmistakable tone of a well-to-do man. If he spoke the truth and was an actual physician, he must be doing charity work.

The medical profession in England was divided into three layers of care. At the bottom was the apothecary, who mixed drugs and looked after the poor.

Next was the surgeon, who did the manual work, such as setting broken bones.

At the peak of the hierarchy was the physician, the gentlemen's doctor. University-trained and a member of the Royal College of Physicians, he would listen to your chest, prescribe a nostrum, and charge you twenty pounds for the pleasure.

A physician would not lower himself to attend to patients needing boils lanced or to offer aid to a prostitute with venereal disease.

What was this man doing in the bowels of the earth attending to the underprivileged?

"Sister Monica claims you are unwell? Could you describe what's wrong?" he asked.

A coughing fit overtook her, which undoubtedly summed up her current health. Even she could hear the rattle in her chest.

The doctor leaned in, the stethoscope held in his gloved hand. "May I?"

Pulling aside the collar of her frayed blouse, he listened to her chest. "Take deep breaths and exhale."

"Pneumonia?" she asked.

The doctor gave her a look as if astounded. "A correct diagnosis. A mild case. You shall remain here for five days, keep warm and fed, rest, and drink plenty of fluids, and the congestion in your lungs should lessen. In the meantime, Sister Monica will take your history and ascertain how we can assist you. Do you have any medical knowledge?"

It took all her inner strength to hide the look of panic. She'd given too much away.

Biting her lower lip, she shook her head. "No. My—mother died of something similar. Weak lungs run in the family."

At least that was not a lie.

"But you do have some education? I ask as your speech indicates such, as does your clothing."

Despite the threadbare condition of her clothes, they revealed her once middle-class standing—or former standing.

"A little schooling," she replied wearily.

"You're exhausted. We have a pallet and blanket for you. Come, I will assist you with it, and you can rest. Sister Monica will give you willow bark tea when you awake to relieve your slight fever."

He reached for her bundle, but she cried out and clutched it tightly. These few items were all she had, and no one would take them from her.

"I'm sorry. I will not touch your belongings. Will you allow me to take your arm?" the doctor asked gently.

His voice was soft and deep, his eyes kind and solicitous. Why couldn't Lydia have met a man like this instead of John Huntsford? Tonight was not the time to contemplate her many errors in judgment or think about how she loathed being a victim. But she is a victim of her own hubris and selfishness.

She nodded, and the doctor helped her to a pallet near one of the stoves. Once the doctor assisted her to lie on the bench, she again used her bundle as a pillow.

Doctor Damian covered her with a patched but clean blanket, and a soft moan escaped her lips from the sensation of actually lying flat in a modicum of comfort and warmth. Lydia would never take a warm bowl of stew and a place to sleep for granted again.

"Sleep. No one will disturb you the rest of the night. No one will rob you, as volunteers roam the area to keep it safe. I'll come and see you again tomorrow night."

"Thank you, Doctor...."

But he was already gone, like a wisp of smoke.

Lydia's eyelids lowered, and she fell fast asleep, warm and comfortable for the first time in weeks.

And more importantly, she felt—safe.

Chapter 3

"DOCTOR DAMIAN, MAY I see you for a moment?"

Harrison followed Sister Monica to the small makeshift office they had arranged in the corner, consisting of eight-foot-tall planks acting as walls and a temporary door. Once they found themselves alone, he tore off his mask and cap. Besides Sister Monica, only Sister Agatha knew his true identity.

"My lord, you've been here five hours without a break. I insist you sit, and I'll bring you a bowl of ham stew and a piece of bread while we discuss the summaries."

"You have a valid point, Sister. The stew and bread are welcome." With a weary sigh, Harrison flopped onto the old desk chair.

He peeled off the silk gloves and tossed them on the desk. He'd fashioned them from a pair of ladies cut down from elbow length to a few inches above the wrist. They were damned awkward but protected his hands from various diseases and astringents. Since they were a lady's size, the tight fit allowed some measure of dexterity.

Sister Monica departed to fetch the stew, and he overheard her ask one of the men to stand watch outside the flimsy door to ensure his privacy.

Harrison acted as Doctor Damian for five years.

He would admonish himself for being such a coward when he was in a low mood. However, hiding his identity was the only way Harrison could practice the type of medicine he'd always wanted without any outside comment or interference. Or judgment.

Society would never accept a marquess and heir to a duke as a doctor, not even as a gentleman's physician. It was damned unfair and entirely idiotic. But that didn't impede him from studying medicine at Cambridge.

At university, his fellow students thought him mad. Eccentric.

That *word* again.

Perhaps his entire family was mad. Regardless, he lived this secret life longer than he cared to count. It all started eleven years past when he took a trip to the Scottish Highlands, not for a restful holiday but to live in a remote village and act as their surgeon for two months. The experience had been so rewarding that he made other such extended journeys to the far-flung corners of Great Britain.

To his family and the outside world, he was a rake and a selfish, entitled peer who traveled aimlessly, indulging in the worst vices. He cultivated the fabrication, and besides the two nuns, only his close friend from Cambridge, Samuel Kenward—who believed in providing medical treatment for the poor the same as him—knew of his secret life.

Keeping it quiet had become tedious and more difficult as the years passed. Harrison's aristocratic background had caught up with him. Since he was a man of duty to his very core, he could no longer neglect the responsibilities of being an heir to a duke.

Hell, not even his brothers knew; they were his close friends besides his siblings. Harrison had no doubt they would support him in his covert endeavors. Yet, he decided long ago, to protect his family from further gossip, it was better not to divulge anything.

In moments of reflection, he often wondered if he'd made the right decision in keeping this secret.

Yes, he most definitely was a coward.

But Harrison also wanted to live his life on his terms. At least as much as the strictures of society and the aristocracy allowed.

Sister Monica burst through the door carrying a tray. "I made you a cup of tea and slipped in a nip of Irish whiskey."

Harrison rubbed his hands together in anticipation. "You are a true saint, Sister."

She laid the tray before him and reached for a mug of tea. Knowing the nun, she doubtless added whiskey to her cup. Taking a sip as she pulled the stool closer to his plank desk, Harrison tucked into the meal, hungrier than he first thought.

"Right you are; you eat and listen while I talk, my lord. The clinic is full. Word is spreading farther out onto the streets, and we will have to start turning people away or shorten the time they stay at the terminus."

She took another sip, smiling with satisfaction at the whiskey burn. "Oh, that's good, that is. Anyway, back to the report. Word is not only getting out to those in need. A baron's son asked if he could volunteer a few nights a week. Well, you could have knocked me over with a feather. I said yes; how could I turn away help?"

"What name did he give?" Harrison asked between spoonfuls of soup.

"Cyril Bottomly. Son of Baron Jacob Bottomly."

"I've heard of the baron, and he does have a son. What chores did you assign to him?"

"The young man ladled out the soup, helped move some pallets, took the dirty laundry to the church, and brought clean blankets in return. He asked if he could return in a few days. I agreed, of course. Who knows whether he is doing some self-imposed penance or has an altruistic reason?"

Interesting.

"Give him more to do, and if anyone else asks to volunteer, use your judgment. You're a fine arbitrator of a person's character. Use your discretion."

The nun sighed. "How much longer can we get away with this, my lord? Why haven't we been shut down?"

Harrison tore off a piece of bread. "Because we serve a purpose, and it's not costing the British government anything, they allow us to exist as long as we remain somewhat secret."

"Ah. Cost. Now we come to the heart of it. My lord, I know this is none of my business, but you cannot continue to fund this place with your money. It isn't proper. It was one thing when we had several dozen on any given night, but now it is in the hundreds. The cost must be great."

"You're correct, Sister. It *is* none of your business. How I choose to spend my inheritance is my concern." Harrison's words were clipped, his tone harsh.

But Sister Monica was made of sterner stuff. She met his angry gaze and jutted out her chin in defiance. "It may be none of my concern, my lord, but I worry for you toiling away down here hours at a time, night after night. Someone has to speak the truth to you and care about your welfare. Because the great cost is not only money but your physical and mental health."

His irritation dissipated. Sister Monica was right, and he was grateful for her concern.

"Please accept my apologies for my curt response. Blame it on weariness and frustration. I told you to call me Harrison when we're alone. After five years, I think you can manage it—Monica."

He took a long tea drink, savoring the Irish whiskey's bite. "I'm aware we cannot keep up this pretense much longer. The time has come to take this public and set up a society of sorts and garner the support of benevolent donors. Outdoor relief is increasing at last. There are those working outside the stringent Poor Law Act. I believe we do not need to operate in secret any longer."

Sister Monica frowned. "Harrumph. I don't care for the Charity Organization Society with their draconian methods of determining who are the deserving poor or undeserving poor."

"I completely agree. You have to admit that some take advantage of relief efforts to avoid work. We've seen a few down here and more than once."

"Well, shouldn't that be the government's job? It seems that the government is handing more responsibility to private concerns. Harrison, it's not right."

She finally called him by name, and he smiled. Who would have thought he would become friends with a liberal-thinking nun in her sixties? Harrison admired her and the others for running a soup kitchen clinic outside the scope of the New Poor Law. The problem was that the charitable proposition devoured money. His fortune had been depleted by more than two-thirds in his bid to aid those in need.

There must be a better way.

Also, if he were honest, his health began to suffer. On that point, Sister Monica was utterly correct. He is in a rundown condition, exhausted, running on little sleep and even less food. Harrison dropped eight pounds in the past four months alone. This enterprise was running away from him while completely engulfing his life.

A few years ago, Harrison had been ennobled by Queen Victoria by a writ of acceleration, meaning even though he held the courtesy title, he could attend the House of Lords as a sitting member. It was rare and showed how the queen liked and admired his father. Between sitting in Parliament and his physician duties at night, Harrison was done in, utterly exhausted. Both commitments suffered so much that he had no idea what to do about it.

"I concur," he replied. "Remember, it's the government that ran those horrific workhouses. It took decades of slow incremental change to see even the slightest improvement, which is still insufficient."

Harrison took a spoonful of stew. "Allow me to broach the subject with Sam Kenward, and I will also discuss it with my father. Perhaps a charitable public clinic for those in need may be the answer we seek. A temporary place of reprieve."

"I will leave it in your capable hands. Here are the totals for today," Sister Monica announced. "Fifteen new cases. From the total, seven moved to the tuberculosis infirmary. Two more have started jobs at the docks. A family of six agreed to head to the workhouse on Waterloo Road."

Where they would be separated.

No wonder families chose to live on the street before heading to one of those abominations. As he'd mentioned to Sister Monica, the places had improved since The government decided to house the infirmaries in separate locations, but the conditions were still deplorable in Harrison's view.

As he took another spoonful of the hearty stew, his mind wandered to the young woman with onset pneumonia. Attractive—and he'd no business thinking such under the circumstances. Harrison would hazard to guess her state of affairs was more recent than most due to her mode of clothing, though the garments were worn and dirty.

"The young woman with the golden hair, have you found out her name and situation?"

Sister Monica arched an eyebrow at him. "No, not as yet. I decided to let her sleep since she was dead on her feet. There is time enough tomorrow to question her. Did she touch you in some way?"

A sizzling awareness moved through him when he took her arm like a wave crashing on a shoreline. But that was not what Monica meant. The nun spoke of his heart.

Harrison had learned long ago to keep his heart hidden and well-protected. It was a habit he intended to keep.

"She is not the obvious poor we see down here is the reason," Harrison replied. "The young lady diagnosed herself. Her mode of dress suggests a middle-class upbringing and possible education."

"I'll see to her personally, never fear. She claims not to be a prostitute, and I believe her. She doesn't have the look of the street."

Monica placed her mug on the desk. "Now. You have seen everyone, and most have settled in for the day. After you eat, I insist you return home and rest. We have enough food to see us through to the end of the week and enough chalk lime for the cesspits. Doctor Sam will be here in the morning. So there is no need for you to come again until tomorrow night. Sleep, and eat a hearty breakfast. That is an order, my lord." She gave him a warm smile. "I mean, Harrison."

It wouldn't hurt to follow Monica's instructions. A good night's sleep and a hearty breakfast sounded like a brilliant suggestion.

Yet, he couldn't stop thinking about the young woman.

What was her story? What brought her to such a low point? What caused the weariness and fear he'd seen in her remarkable green-blue eyes?

Shaking the thoughts away, he turned his mind to the upcoming ball.

Now that he was seeking an appropriate bride, perhaps he should retire "Doctor Damian" for good, come out of the shadows, and pour his energy into a more permanent and viable clinic for the underprivileged.

And forget the pretty young woman with the tragic appearance.

Chapter 4

A BABY'S PIERCING CRY woke Lydia with a start. It took several minutes to get her bearings, and she gasped when she found the older nun standing over her.

"You're awake at last. You've slept around the clock. It is half past eleven in the morning. Much needed, I daresay. Before I bring you a meal, we should get you washed up. I recall you saying you've only been on the streets a few days, not long enough to collect any crawlers—lice, fleas, and the like. We'll check you anyhow. Stand up, miss—what's your name?"

Oh. Lydia couldn't give her own; she didn't dare.

"Lucinda Best."

"Miss Best, please follow me. You may bring your bundle."

Lydia accompanied the nun, and behind the screen was a basin filled with water, and next to it lay small towels and a bar of soap.

"All you can manage is a sponge bath, but I encourage you to wash all the bits you can. No one will disturb you. Then we shall check you for any unwanted visitors. Are you able to stand?" Sister Monica asked.

Though her legs were shaky, she nodded.

"It's a rough carbolic soap, but it will get you clean enough. I'll leave you to it."

The nun bustled away, and Lydia slowly peeled off her tattered coat, small jacket, and blouse. Dipping her hands in the basin, she gasped at the pleasant sensation of warm water. How long had it been since Lydia had a proper wash?

Once she lowered the straps on her bodice, she quickly soaped up the small flannel and commenced washing the grime of the streets away. Too bad she could not scrub the horrid memories of the past months.

Caught up in her chore, Lydia didn't hear the nun enter the cramped area. She cried out when Sister Monica grabbed her arm, turning it upright. Lydia slapped her hand over the needle marks at the bend of her elbow.

"How recent are those?" The nun asked, her tone brisk.

Lydia yanked her arm out of Sister Monica's grip. "Not recent."

The nun arched an eyebrow but did not comment. She gave Lydia a dubious look.

"I am telling the truth," Lydia said firmly.

"When finished, return to your pallet. We will be discussing your situation. Hurry along."

Her face flushing, Lydia admonished herself for coming here. If she'd known she'd get an interrogation rivaling a hardened Scotland Yard detective, she would have taken her chances and stayed in the alley, shivering behind the crates and barrels.

A wave of dizziness overcame her, and she clasped the ends of the table to steady her trembling body. No, Lydia was quite ill. If she stayed out of doors, she'd have succumbed, of that she had no doubt.

After swiping the soapy cloth under her arm, her mind tried to formulate a story that would satisfy the meddlesome nun. Lydia hated lying, but her recent history was no one's business.

But instead of crafting a suitable fable, her thoughts drifted to the angel of medical mercy with the mesmerizing silver-gray eyes.

Lord, his touch.

Even through the gloves and her garments, Lydia felt a surge of sensual awareness she had never experienced at her initial meeting with John Huntsford. At least not right away. Huntsford charmed her. Eventually, she developed feelings toward him.

In no time, Lydia fell under Surgeon Huntsford's spell. Because of it, she had done anything that he asked. Everything that he had demanded.

Apparently, she possessed a weakness for men of medicine.

More than likely, the liability was far graver than handsome doctors. Not an easy admission as Lydia prided herself on her independence, but underneath the truth laid the fact that she was lonely. When John Huntsford paid her the slightest bit of attention, she imagined she was in love.

More fool her.

No, she would not think of it or reveal any of it to a strange nun. Stick to the truth as much as possible, but leave out Mr. Huntsford and her tenure as a nurse.

Rinsing off, she quickly dressed, grabbed her bundle, and unsteadily made her way to her pallet. Sure enough, the nun stood by, holding an enamel mug.

"Let us sit on this makeshift bench. Here, it's tea with willow bark. I'll bring your meal after our discussion. Doctor Damian believes you have some education and a middle-class background, correct?"

Lydia's eyes welled with tears thinking of her late father, a gentle, scholarly man who provided a loving home. She blinked them away. It was best not to show too much emotion, as others perceived it as a weakness.

"Yes. My father was a schoolmaster. He died, and I have no one else. What little money left to me has run out." So far, she'd told the truth—more or less. "I haven't been able to find suitable work, and before I knew it, I was on the street."

"And the marks on your arm?"

Lydia frowned as she sipped the tea. "I will not discuss it. A temporary lapse in judgment is all I will say on the matter."

"Is that where your money disappeared—into your arm?" The nun's voice was gentle, coaxing, and even empathetic, considering the evidence of her drug use.

It was not strictly the truth, but Lydia nodded, drinking more tea, savoring the warmth moving through her.

"I'll bring you food, and after, we'll do a quick check for crawlers. Then you must put your feet up, Miss Best. You're still flushed, and the rattle in your chest is audible with each breath you take. Doctor Damian will examine you tonight and may have more questions for you. Drink your tea."

The nurse stood and headed to the stoves, leaving Lydia to exhale in relief.

She managed to slip past the first hurdle.

Though a part of her dreaded further questioning from the angel doctor, another part leaped in anticipation of being near him again. Close enough to watch his attractive eyes study her intently as if trying to make her out. Imagine what features he hid behind his all-white garments. What color was his hair? It was hard to tell as his eyebrows were hidden under the white cap.

No matter.

She had no business imagining anything about Doctor Damian, not after her wretched and twisted relationship with Surgeon Huntsford.

Lydia would do well to remember it.

Chapter 5

THE RESTORATIVE POWERS of a good night's rest never ceased to amaze Harrison, and waking refreshed also worked wonders for his appetite. He consumed two full plates of breakfast as he read his collection of newspapers, including *The Daily Telegraph* and *The Times*. The quiet time was a brief respite in his demanding life, and Harrison made a mental note to do this more often.

He stayed in his town house on Marylebone Road, a few streets away from his father's city residence in Mayfair. Still an affluent area, Marylebone afforded him a degree of privacy, and its central London location made any part of the city accessible.

Harrison's dwelling was modest compared to the Duke of Gransford's residence, which had been in the family since the early 1700s. Harrison kept the household staff to the bare minimum with two maids-of-all-work, a cook, housekeeper, under-butler, footman, and Gillis, his personal valet.

Harrison never cared for ostentatiousness, which he could hardly avoid with his family's revered standing.

The seaside marquess manor in Eastbourne had been in the family for decades, and Harrison spent part of his childhood there until his father became the duke when Harrison was six years old. For five years, Harrison made this town house his permanent home. He rarely traveled to the family estate, Gransford Manor, in Hastings, or his estate in Eastbourne.

The double doors opened, and Youngston, the under-butler, entered. One day Youngston will replace his father's aging butler. Youngston joined the Gransford estate as an orphaned boy, became a gardener's assistant, and worked his way into the household staff and up the ranks. At thirty-eight, the tall, elegant Youngston made for an impressive presence, and Harrison could not remember a time he'd not been around.

He'd chosen his staff carefully, trusted people in his father's employ for decades. Harrison was not aware if his servants knew of his secrets, but one thing he did know? They would never gossip about him outside these walls. Of that, he was sure.

"Doctor Kenward to see you, my lord. Shall I have him wait in your study?"

Harrison set his teacup on the saucer. "No, have him join me here. I'm sure he's famished." He turned slightly toward the young footman. "Harris, you may leave us."

"Will you be attending Parliament this afternoon, my lord?" Youngston asked.

"Yes, then I have appointments this evening. Do not wait up for me. Inform Gillis, will you?"

"Very well, my lord."

Bowing, Youngston and Harris departed as Sam Kenward strode into the dining room, rubbing his hands together as he spotted the chafing dishes on the sideboard.

"Brilliant. I hoped I arrived in time for breakfast."

Sam hummed an innocuous tune as he loaded his plate with curried eggs, ham, fresh fruit, and pastries. Once he set his plate on the table, he poured himself a cup of coffee and sat opposite Harrison.

"Have you been to the terminus?" Harrison asked as he set aside his newspapers.

"Briefly. Four new people this morning. There was no place to put them, so I asked Sister Agatha to see who was ready to leave and to speed up their departures. It's getting well out of hand. We cannot keep up with the steady and never-ending influx of those in need." Sam stuffed a morsel of eggs in his mouth.

"Yes. Sister Monica and I were speaking of the same issue. Let's consider making the soup kitchen clinic public. We cannot keep up this punishing pace—either of us or the nuns. Perhaps we'd better find a permanent location near the church so the nuns can keep a hand in."

Harrison bit into his toast. "It will mean setting up a charitable society," he said in-between bites. "Finding affluent donors. And what better way to do such than at a fancy ball?"

Sam frowned. "I cannot go to such an event." Harrison raised an eyebrow in question. "Come now; I'm barely middle class. I could only go to Cambridge through the generosity of Squire Robinson, a prominent landowner in my village. Besides, I do not fit in with upper-crust peers and their ilk. You know this."

"We are friends."

Sam chuckled as he cut his ham. "As if that alone is reason enough for me to attend. You're different and always were. You never had any airs. Neither did your brothers. Considering that you are sons of a prominent and wealthy duke, I am astounded."

"I have airs. I manage to fight most of those selfish impulses. But it is not always successful."

Sam scoffed at his assessment, but it was true. Anyone privileged was susceptible to such behavior.

"For all my parents' aristocratic blood, they are firm believers in charity work and helping those less fortunate," Harrison continued. "They instilled those values in all of us. Unfortunately, Spence's unique and dissimilar personality does not translate well to social situations, but he contributed in other ways. Mostly of the monetary persuasion."

"I never understood why you haven't informed your family of your charity works these past years. Surely, they could have contributed to your clinic and encouraged others to do so. Or will you tell me to mind my own business?" Sam's mouth quirked.

How could Harrison explain?

Though his parents never pressured him, especially about carrying on the line, he felt it nonetheless. It was something only an heir to a duke would understand. The responsibility was ponderous and no doubt of his own making. It weighed heavily. But he had decided when he came of age to fuel the talk of his being a rake.

Society forgave an heir to a duke for being a rake, for it was expected and, in some corners, even admired. It allowed him to live a surreptitious life and protect his family from censure in the bargain.

Helping people experiencing poverty was not.

It was a sad statement about the upper classes and society in general.

"I wanted to accomplish something on my own, to practice medicine *my* way," Harrison explained softly. "My family had to endure enough interest and speculation over the years. The last thing I wish to do is to add to it, especially with the gossip about Tremain making the rounds as of late. Acting as a rake causes much less speculation."

Harrison took a sip of tea and continued. "Tremain served as a vicar for more than two years. My brother has great plans for the village of Hawksgreen regarding education and other reforms. Yet, all society can focus on is his so-called war injuries and other salacious tattle with no basis in truth. I cannot stay in the shadows any longer. No law states I cannot be a physician and practice the medicine I wish. If Tremain can find a way to serve his fellowman in a more public venue, then so can I."

Since Tremain recently emerged from the shadows, Harrison had contemplated doing the same. He should have done it sooner.

It was well past time. Harrison had reached a crossroads.

"There is no legal impediment to you being a doctor, but society will frown upon it and judge accordingly. As you said, it is hardly fair, but that is the world we live in. More's the pity," Sam stated as he sipped his coffee. "But I agree you should go public. Tremain realized he could accomplish far more as viscount than a vicar, just as you will accomplish more as marquess and heir to a duke than as a doctor. A dismal reality."

Harrison frowned. Blast it all; why couldn't he do both? Damn society and its snobbish ways. Granted, Sir William Gull, a Baronet, was a Physician-in-Ordinary to Queen Victoria, but Sir William came from a modest, lower-class background. The Queen made Gull a baronet on his ability to treat the Prince of Wales for typhoid fever.

However, no one *born* into the peerage served as a physician in any capacity he was aware of.

Perhaps he could be the first.

"Yes, it is indeed a dismal state of affairs. Regardless, you will accompany me to the ball," Harrison stated firmly. "You're respectable enough. Besides, you will be there as my guest. In between dances with eligible young ladies, we can assess the aristocracy and decide who would be amenable to supporting a medical charity clinic. After breakfast, Gillis can fit you into one of my suits. We have similar builds; altering it will not take much."

Sam sneered. "When is this blasted event?"

"Barely a week away. Next Friday evening. After the fitting, we will discuss this clinic idea further before I depart for Westminster for the afternoon session. I will broach the subject with Father when I head to Gransford Manor for the weddings in three and a half weeks." Harrison reached for an iced bun from the nearby platter.

"Do give my best to your brothers," Sam offered as he took another bite of ham.

The two of them were making short work of the remaining breakfast food.

Harrison nodded. "I will. Only family in attendance. Spence insisted."

"I surmised as much." Sam continued to eat heartily. He said between bites, "Are you going to the Terminus tonight?"

"Yes. Only for a couple of hours."

More than anything, Harrison wished to see the mysterious young lady again and hear her story. Assist her in any way he could.

No woman had caught his attention like this before.

She even invaded his dreams last night, some erotic doings to be sure, but Miss Best also invaded the part of his heart he kept well hidden, stoking his protective instincts to unknown levels. Damned unsettling, but it also caused him to feel more alive in years.

Caution was in order.

He had a strict and implacable plan for his future, and it didn't include a downtrodden woman, no matter how she appealed.

Harrison inwardly winced. God, that sounded arrogant to his own ears. As he had just observed to Sam, the instinct for snobbish impulses and thoughts was there.

From what he observed, Miss Best possessed inner strength. To find herself in such reduced circumstances, to place pride aside and seek assistance? To Harrison, that took courage, and he admired her, which made her all the more intriguing.

No. Harrison must remain detached in their dealings.

As difficult as that may be.

Chapter 6

AFTER A HUMILIATING inspection for crawlers, as Sister Monica called them, her meal, and sleeping on and off throughout the day, Lydia could claim to feel marginally better. Except for the rattle in her chest remained. Her muscles and joints ached terribly, and the fever lingered, though, at the end of the five days, she would be past the worst of it.

Then what to do? Where to go?

How much to reveal to the well-meaning nun and the mysterious Doctor Damian? How could she place her trust in anyone ever again?

Sitting upright on her pallet with the blanket about her shoulders, she opened her bundle. Within were a few personal items she managed to gather before her late-night flight from the shabby rooms she shared with Huntsford: a silver hairbrush, originally her mother's, and a silver butterfly hair comb. Lydia ran her fingers across her treasures.

In truth, she may have to sell them to start over, but what would they be worth? A couple of pounds if she was lucky.

Also, inside the bundle were two starched blouses, a woolen scarf, and a chemise, which she refused to wear as long as she was homeless.

Tears welled as soon as she pulled out the book *Republic* by Plato. It had belonged to her schoolmaster father. He'd encouraged her to pursue a career in nursing.

"My dear girl, you must make your way in the world. I will not be here forever; then what will become of you? Learn all you can, read, absorb knowledge; only then will you gain wisdom."

A lot of good the sage advice had done her.

Her father's lessons, gentle direction, and sagacious guidance were all for naught. Where was that hard-earned wisdom when she needed it the most? She hugged the book tight to her chest, allowing the indulgence of a few tears.

"Miss Best?"

Oh, Lord. It's him.

There was no mistaking the smooth-as-silk, masculine tones. Quickly wiping away the lone tear that trickled down her cheek, Lydia stuffed the book and other items in her bundle and pushed them behind her.

"Doctor Damian. Good afternoon."

He lowered to his haunches. "Are you in distress?"

Having him this close afforded her a better look at his stunning eyes. Long black lashes spiked out from his lids. It could mean his hair was black, but not necessarily. The dark lashes only enhanced the silver-gray of the pupil. How unique and attractive. Struck afresh at his potent presence, she looked away.

"No more than anyone else here. Perhaps less so."

It was then Lydia realized he spoke the name she gave the nun. Which also meant the woman told him everything.

"All is not lost, Miss Best. In seeking out help, you have taken the first step on the road to recovery. I'm not only speaking of your health. Would you mind if we sat on this nearby bench?" He stood and held out a gloved hand.

She slipped her hand into his with a huff and immediately engulfed with a comforting warmth. He assisted her in getting to her feet, and when he released her hand, she immediately missed his touch.

Once seated, he turned slightly to face her. "I wish to examine the needle marks on your arm. Would you permit me?"

Blast it all.

Ashamed, she tore off her wool coat and jacket and pushed up the sleeve of her blouse. Holding her arm face up, she looked away, not wanting to see the look of censure in his eyes.

With a gentle touch, he ran his gloved fingers across the scarring. "These are not recent. How long ago?"

Lydia gulped. "More than three months."

"Opium or cocaine?"

"A mixture of both, I imagine."

"Toxic and dangerous. Did you become addicted?"

Lydia met his gaze. There was no judgment anywhere in his eyes, only concern. When was the last time someone worried for her? Her poor, dear father.

"No. I don't crave it."

His fingers continued to explore the bumps. "The skin was torn during the injecting; did you do this, or did someone else?"

Doctor Damian wandered too close to the truth. No matter his conciliatory tone, she would not reveal the depths of her debauched relationship with Huntsford to anyone.

She yanked her arm away and pulled the sleeve down to cover the scars.

"It's in the past, one I would rather forget." A coughing fit overtook her, and she brought up phlegm in her hand. How mortifying.

But the doctor did not react; merely pulled a cloth from his apron pocket, clasped her hand, and wiped it.

"Yellow," he murmured. "A sign of an infection. But you know that, do you not, Miss Best?"

"Only because my mother died of consumption, Doctor," she replied firmly.

He folded the cloth and tucked it away. "The medical term generally used now is tuberculosis, but I believe you already know. How long ago did your mother succumb to her ailment?"

"Ten years past."

"Sister Monica mentioned that since your father's death, you've been alone and have run out of money. Would you be open to considering a job?"

Oh, why couldn't everyone leave her alone?

She was an ungrateful piece of baggage. Lydia was in no position to turn down assistance. Not at this stage. It is why she came here, after all. Well, for medical aid more than anything, but she might as well accept the help. There were no other options.

"Doing what?" she sniffled.

The doctor handed her another cloth, and she wiped her runny nose.

"When you've recovered, we could procure a position in a shop. Or perhaps a companion to a lady."

Companion? Indentured servant more like.

But Lydia could not be choosy. Being a companion meant she would be off the street, hidden away.

"I thought that particular job was out of fashion, belonging to another era."

"Perhaps, but some older ladies still wish for a companion."

"The way I look?"

"One step at a time, Miss Best. It would help if you recovered first. We have donations of second-hand clothes. There may be something that will suffice for an interview. We not only give aid medically and physically, but we also assist—those who wish it—another chance to rejoin society in whatever capacity."

Doctor Damian stood. "Yes. Working as a companion would suit a young lady like yourself. You are well-spoken, educated, and have experience caring for someone ill."

A young lady such as yourself.

Well. The doctor put her in her place. Servant, indeed.

Lydia's nerves were raw and worn to a tiny nub. Her emotions tumbled in all directions, and her reactions were unpredictable. But judging by the kindness she read in the doctor's eyes, he meant no insult, and she should not take it as one.

"You've had your dinner?" he asked.

Lydia nodded, pulling the blanket closer about her shoulders.

"We do not have much of a varied menu. Mostly stews of whatever meat we can procure and bread of varying degrees of freshness and the occasional apple."

"It tasted heavenly. I am very grateful."

"Then I will instruct Sister Monica to bring you elderflower water with two drops of laudanum. The elderflower will ease your sore throat, and the laudanum will help you relax and sleep." He paused. "You've no issues with laudanum?"

Did he think her a drug fiend?

Annoyance made her bristle, but considering the marks on her arm, what else was the man to think? As Lydia observed, her emotions were all over the place.

"No issues."

"Very well. Rest. I will check on you tomorrow."

Doctor Damian barely stepped away from her when a clamor rose nearby.

A man yelled, "Coppers! Leg it, or they'll take ye away!"

Police? Here?

Panic settled deep inside her, causing her skin to prickle. Grabbing her bundle, Lydia stood, as did others who could manage it.

Doctor Damian strode toward a man in a bowler hat, wearing an outrageous plaid suit. He stood near one of the nuns. Lydia inched closer to investigate the commotion.

The surrounding crowd buzzed with a mixture of excitement and apprehension.

One woman beside her said, "Well, that's it. Mark my words, this place will shut down, and all of us 'auled off to the nick."

Prison? Dear God. No.

Fear gripped Lydia, her insides twisting in a knot.

"This is Doctor Damian," the nun declared. "You speak to him."

The copper had a weasel face and a long nose. Already Lydia did not like the look of him.

"Detective Constable Willis, with the Metropolitan Police. I'm investigating a pharmaceutical theft from St. Thomas Hospital. One of the suspects has done a runner, and I'm checking various places the young lady might be hiding."

Lydia's heart banged against her ribcage in alarm.

St. Thomas. It is where she trained.

Where she worked—with John Huntsford.

"Before we go any further, do you have an identification card?" Doctor Damian asked, his tone cold and officious.

DC Willis handed one to the doctor.

"This card says G Division, in King's Cross. Aren't you a little off your track?"

The detective sniffed. "This case is a top priority, and because of it, all divisions are taking it on. I am seeking a nurse by the name of Lydia Chesterton. Has anyone with that name meandered in here recently? Young and pretty she is, with golden hair. She's wanted for questioning."

Lydia gasped. They were looking for her.

Blast Huntsford, he must have gone through with his miserable scheme and pointed the finger at her. Lydia knew this would happen, which was one reason for her hasty departure. She wanted nothing to do with any theft, but it turns out she was part of it anyway. And her getaway made her look all the more guilty—another foolish decision to add to her shameful list of mistakes.

Doctor Damian handed the card to the copper. "No one with that name here, though; who is to say people give us the correct names? I respect my patient's privacy."

"Then you won't object to me having a look for myself for anyone fitting the description."

The crowd grew restless, and the murmurs became louder. There were probably more people than her down here hiding from society.

Hiding from the law.

"I do object," the doctor replied firmly. "There are many sick people and young children here, and they should not be alarmed."

The copper glanced about. "You're aware this place is illegal? All soup kitchens do is attract vagrants and criminals and outlawed for that reason."

The doctor crossed his arms. "You would haul in well-meaning nuns, Sisters in Christ, for providing a bowl of stew to the destitute?"

The detective rubbed the back of his neck. "Well, maybe not the good sisters, but I'd take you in without hesitation. Legally, I can close this underground charity. And I will unless you allow me to walk about."

Lydia heard enough. So had many others as a few men shoved their way through the crowd.

"You won't be takin' me, copper!" one bellowed as he headed toward the tunnel exit. Somebody shoved an older lady to the ground, and a man punched one of the panicking people. More shoving, yelling, and fisticuffs ensued. All hell broke loose.

It turned the detective's attention and the doctor and nun toward the growing fracas. Lydia used the opportunity to slip away. As she skirted past some empty pallets, she tucked her bundle under her arm, shamelessly grabbed pieces of bread and an apple with her free hands, and ran.

She didn't stop running until she was out through the makeshift door and five streets away. Out of breath and wheezing, Lydia ducked into a dark alley and stood against the wall, hidden in the shadows.

Once again, she was on her own.

It was then she realized the blanket still hung about her shoulders. Staring down at the food in her hand, she realized she was a thief in reality.

A lone, desolate sob escaped her throat as she placed the food in her bundle. Briefly, she was allowed to hope. To believe that she could start over and be someone else.

Now that she knew the police were seeking her—and probably Huntsford was also looking for her—Lydia had no choice but to depart London immediately. But how?

Fatigue washed over her as another coughing fit wracked her body. But not tonight.

Feeling her way down the dark alley, she found crates piled up in the corner. Wedging behind them, she curled against the bricks, pulling the blanket tight about her.

For a fleeting moment, people were kind to her and offered her assistance and compassion. For a few precious hours, she felt—safe.

Lydia would never look into those caring and beautiful silver-gray eyes again, and the thought tore her heart in two.

Chapter 7

AS HARRISON SPUN THE Honorable Miss Nicola Westbank about the ballroom, the cloying scent of lilies of the valley filled his nostrils. The girl was no more than eighteen or nineteen years of age, much too young for him. After taking stock of the eligible ladies at this dance, Harrison concluded that he'd waited far too late to enter the so-called marriage mart.

Usually, a man of his advancing age would pick a bride this young strictly for breeding purposes. God, what a horrible thought, and it wasn't his observation, not at all. But it is what the elite of society called it, as if the unfortunate young women had no other purpose.

Perhaps a tiny part of him still hoped love would enter the equation. The thoughts of sharing his life with a simpering, giggling girl made his insides churn.

Harrison glanced down into the hopeful face of Miss Westbank, who smiled shyly at him. Pretty enough, she barely spoke—merely flushed in reply to his inane utterances. He'd long since run out of small talk. As a result, his mind started to wander as he continued to waltz across the dance floor.

As he had many times the past five days, he thought of Miss Best and her mysterious disappearance. To leave while the detective was there spoke of a more serious reason for her homelessness.

Was she the woman that the detective sought? The physical description certainly fits.

Why the distraught Miss Best kept entering his thoughts—and his dreams, for that matter— puzzled as much as concerned him.

Accept it; she's gone.

Harrison wished he'd helped her in the way that she needed. After the commotion had died after the detective's visit, it was over an hour before he realized Miss Best was missing. He sent two volunteers into the surrounding streets to look for her, but they came up empty.

People around him were clapping, so he ceased dancing and did the same. Offering his arm, he swiftly escorted the girl to her parents, Viscount and Countess Roland. Once he reached the party, he bowed slightly and turned to leave.

"One moment if you please, Lord Tennington," the countess sniffed, "Whom is that young man accompanying you?"

Here we go.

"Doctor Samuel Kenward, we attended Cambridge together."

"Indeed? I do not recall a family with the name of Kenward."

Meaning amongst the aristocrats and wealthy upper crust.

It was a struggle to keep his distaste from outwardly showing. "I do not doubt it."

He bowed again, hoping to make his escape, but the detestable woman latched onto his arm.

"I was always of the opinion that the lower classes should know their place, even in these enlightened times." She gave Harrison a cruel smile.

An insult. A direct hit on Sam.

God, he despised his own class.

Her husband, the viscount, cleared his throat and said, "Quite right."

"'Are there no prisons? Are there no workhouses?' I am paraphrasing the author, Charles Dickens, in case you were unaware," Harrison replied curtly.

A woman standing next to the countess tsked. "That reprehensible man. His scandalous stories have ruined modern literature. Subversive claptrap."

"While his books are compelling," Harrison stated, ignoring the comment, "It is the moral lessons in his tales that resonate. He championed reform concerning economic and social issues. I admired him for it."

"If Dickens had his way, there would be no lines between the classes. The very fabric of English life would unravel," the viscount retorted.

He would not find any contributors to his charity clinic in this arrogant crowd—blasted snobs.

"I agree with the late author," Harrison replied. "There is a need for further reform, and it is up to us, the wealthy and privileged, to lead by example and exhibit a greater understanding and humanitarianism toward the disadvantaged and vulnerable."

A few people standing nearby shifted uncomfortably at his frank but true statement. The rich did not like anyone reminding them that people suffered and struggled with life outside these gilded walls.

"Oh, come now, my lord," Lady Roland retorted. "There are lines between the classes for a reason. For example, allowing them into a social event such as this will spread filth and disease. Of course, I am not speaking of your Cambridge companion."

Again, the countess gave him a smirk befitting a loathsome character in a Dickens novel. "Also, one should not marry into the lower classes either. It weakens the blood. Tarnishes the line. Do you not agree, my dear marquess?"

A slam toward his brothers. His entire family.

Harrison's anger flared, and by Miss Westbank's startled and fearful reaction, his face must look thunderous.

"I welcome and approve of my brothers' choices of a bride, as do my parents, the Duke and Duchess of Gransford. It seems to me that many bloodlines amongst the peerage are overbred, producing frail simpletons with aggressive tendencies. But then, I am not speaking of anyone here." Harrison brushed off Lady Roland's hand and bowed. "If you will excuse me."

He turned on his heel and marched away, with Lady Roland's words, "How dare he?" hanging in the air.

Enough of this dog and pony show.

With a quick visual sweep of the ballroom, he located Sam talking to a young woman on the opposite side. With its stifling heat and even more oppressive company, this event had lost his interest.

His gaze fell upon Lord Shaftesbury sitting in an overstuffed chair. Good lord, the man was in his eighties; why venture out?

The earl was a particular hero of Harrison's, a reformist and a true progressive. Throughout the past decades, the earl oversaw child labor, factory reform, and improvements in education. He should leave the man in peace, but Harrison refused to leave this miserable ball without speaking to at least one peer of worth.

"Good evening, my lord. Harrison Hornsby, Marquess of Tennington. Do you mind if I sit?"

The earl peered over the top of his spectacles. "Gransford's heir? Please take a seat, my lad. I have great respect for your father and his good works. We need more like him in the House of Lords. I must say I am pleased you follow in his footsteps. I quite enjoyed your grand speech on medical reform last autumn. Well done."

Harrison pulled his chair around to face the earl. "Thank you, my lord. It is that very medical reform about which I wish to speak. I promise not to take up much of your time."

"Then be swift and sure in your converse, Lord Tennington." The earl leaned forward on his cane, giving Harrison his full attention.

"I am about to embark on a mission to set up a charity medical clinic. As you know, infirmaries turn away the truly destitute. I wish to have a place of safety, the last resort for those in need. All trained nurses, the nuns of St. Dunstan's Church in Stepney, will serve with a colleague and me in this clinic. At least until the place is running properly."

The earl arched an eyebrow. "You, a marquess?"

"I'm a trained physician, my lord. Unfortunately, I cannot practice except in the most clandestine ways."

A slow smile crept across the earl's face. "Still waters run deep, Tennington. Color me impressed. Is your father aware of your charity work?"

Harrison shook his head. "No, but I will inform him when I travel to the manor at the end of this month. Would you be interested in such a proposal?"

"I am. I came to London for the session but will return to Essex in two weeks. My lungs cannot tolerate this foul London air. Seek me out the day after next at Westminster—three in the afternoon on the terrace. I believe we will have a good deal to discuss. I will also ask the Earl of Carnstone to attend."

Harrison knew him slightly. Julian Wollstonecraft, the Earl of Carnstone, was also well into his eighties but in better health than Shaftesbury. The two men worked side-by-side for decades on various reforms and bills. Carnstone was also a resilient, progressive voice in the House of Lords.

Harrison stood, held out his hand, and the earl took it. "I appreciate it, my lord. Enjoy the rest of your evening."

He snorted. "At this ball? That is not very likely. I only came to please my wife and granddaughter."

Smiling, he bowed, then headed toward Sam with an extra spring in his step.

Tonight was not a complete loss.

Chapter 8

AFTER DROPPING SAM at his flat, Harrison headed to Pratt's at Park Place. He was a member and decided a game of billiards and perhaps a drink or two would help him unwind and dismiss that distasteful conversation with those arrogant, ignorant peers. Thank God not all was lost, considering his pleasanter discussion with the Earl of Shaftsbury.

Before saying goodnight to Sam, he relayed his productive dialogue with the earl, and they both agreed they were off to a solid start regarding their ambitious plans. Bringing his father and brothers on board would only strengthen the cause. With Shaftsbury in their corner and possibly Carnstone, they could line up several more aristocrats and wealthy businesspeople to support their venture.

Now past two in the morning and feeling more than slightly fuzzy-headed from the brandy at Pratt's, he instructed the carriage driver to take him to Stepney High Street. Since he was wide awake, Harrison might as well check in at the terminus. At this time of night, one of the nuns would be there along with the trusted volunteers who kept the underground clinic safe.

The only sound he could hear was the clop-clop of the horses' hooves against the cobbles, though judging by the odor, he must be in the East End. Though not as rank as in previous decades, the sewer smell still permeated the air.

Harrison felt he had accomplished something worthwhile thanks to his conversation with Shaftesbury. Yes, the nights he toiled away at the terminus were also rewarding, but the never-ending stream of poor and sick people could be disheartening.

Damn, the sickeningly sweet punch he consumed at the ball and the three brandies at the club took their toll. Harrison banged on the roof with his walking stick, abruptly stopping the vehicle.

The window slid open. "Yes, my lord?"

"Stop at the next alley you see; I have a call of nature."

"There is one to your right, my lord."

Harrison pushed aside the curtain. From the flickering luminance of the gaslight, he spotted the alley the driver spoke of.

"I will be but a moment. I can manage the steps."

He unfolded the metal steps and descended from the carriage. Sprinting across the cobbles, he entered the alley and, upon finding it empty, unbuttoned the fall of his trousers and pulled out his prick. The steady stream was indeed a relief.

Something between a groan and a whimper caught his attention. Finishing, he righted his trousers and pulled his cloak across his body.

"Is anyone there?"

Silence.

Harrison walked forward; though it was dark, the lamppost cast enough light that he was able to spot crates piled high in the corner.

Was that a boot peeking out from behind?

Grabbing the top crate, he pushed it aside, and the illumination band fell upon a woman's face in obvious distress.

God above, it's Miss Best!

At her feet lay a rotten apple core and bread crumbs. Her eyes were closed, but she clutched her bundle tight to her chest. The blanket still hung about her shoulders as it had the last time he'd seen her before her disappearance.

Harrison pulled the rest of the crates aside without hesitation, then hooked his elbow under her knees and lifted her into his arms. Her face was pale; perspiration beaded along her hairline. Blood had seeped through one of her tattered gloves. Her breathing was shallow, with an audible wheeze sounding on every exhale.

"Miss Best!"

She did not answer, nor did her eyes flutter.

Harrison ran out into the street. "You there!" he called to the hansom cab driver. "Hop down and get the door."

The man touched his forelock and did as commanded. Harrison placed one foot on the step.

"Forget Stepney High Street; make haste to 43 Marylebone Road. I'll pay you with a gold guinea if you can get us there in less than fifteen minutes."

The driver's face lit up, and he touched his forelock again. "At once, my lord."

The driver closed the door, and with a jarring start, the carriage was off at a brisk clip.

Miss Best lay across his lap. Pushing her hair from her face, Harrison was shocked to see how pale she was. Laying the back of his wrist on her forehead, he frowned. The poor woman was burning up. How severe was the fever? It didn't bear thinking about.

"Why on earth did you run, Miss Best? If that is your name," he whispered. "Are you this mysterious Lydia Chesterton the police are seeking? I believe you may be."

His finger trailed across her cracked lips. Dehydration. No doubt malnutrition.

He pulled off her glove and hissed through his teeth at what he found: a bite, no doubt, from a rat. It had broken the skin and bled.

What are the odds that he alone would find her?

Fate had undoubtedly taken a hand.

Harrison's thoughts drifted to his visit last month with his family and Tremain relaying how he met his future wife, Eliza.

Eliza had been disgracefully kicked out of an earl's house and viciously attacked during her journey. She was robbed and nearly raped by the drivers entrusted with seeing her off the premises. Tremain had found her in a snowbank not far from the vicarage. His brother had described the incident as if he stood as a knight of old, rescuing a maiden in distress.

His brother had initially been attracted to her, though he'd tried to deny it. Tremain explained how it slowly but surely melted his frozen heart and brought alive every emotion long buried, including his overwhelming need to protect her.

There was nothing else Harrison wanted to do than to protect this lovely lady from the severity of life.

Miss Best needed him.

And perhaps, he needed her.

The strength of his protective instinct shocked him.

He had never experienced this with any woman before. As Tremain conveyed, every emotion crackled with newfound life and energy.

Dear God. What to do about it?

The first priority is seeing Miss Best well.

Then, when she was on the road to recovery, he would try to understand what was happening and discover if the attraction was mutual.

Chapter 9

WITH SLOW INCREMENTS, Lydia became aware of her surroundings. At first, the crackling sound of wood burning in the hearth entered her consciousness. Then a rolling warmth moved through her.

Fire. Am I in hell?

She opened her eyes, trying to blink away the haze obscuring her vision.

"At last. You're awake, miss."

Lydia turned slightly and fixed her gaze on the person beside her. An older woman, wearing a simple wool dress and pinafore, sat by the bed, mending a shirt.

Spreading her fingers, the realization that she lay in an actual bed surprised her—a bed with quality linens and blankets.

"Where—wh-wh-," Blast it, her voice was as rough as sandpaper.

"Where are you? Why you are in the London home of the Marquess of Tennington. You've been sick with a fever these two days. Touch and go it was, and no mistake. You were shivering something fierce. His lordship brought you in here in the dead of night. Roused me—I'm the housekeeper, by the way, Mrs. Wickes—and roused Youngston, the under-butler."

Lord, this Mrs. Wickes was a talker. Lydia could barely keep up with the conversation. Her mind was that muddled.

"M-m-my bundle—"

"Never fear. The contents are safe in a drawer. There, in that tall dresser. The staff had to burn the bundle itself along with your clothes. Fleas and the like."

She'd picked up crawlers at last. The alley she had hidden in was utterly disgusting. But she had been too weak to venture farther.

The woman stood and poured a glass of water. "His lordship instructed me that if you were to wake, to make sure you drank two glasses of water before anything else."

Carefully lifting Lydia's head, she held the glass to her lips. "Drink now, miss. Slowly. It's important for your recovery, or so says his lordship."

Too weak to resist, Lydia swallowed the cool water. Mrs. Wickes poured another and patiently waited until Lydia drank it dry. It tasted like ambrosia.

Placing her head gently on the pillow, she exhaled, and before she could draw her next breath, a vicious coughing fit overtook her.

The housekeeper wiped away the mucus from her lips. "Still sick. His lordship did say it would be many days before you would feel better and weeks before the cough left you."

Fussing about the room, Mrs. Wickes nodded. "I must return to the kitchen. You rest. Sleep. His lordship is at Parliament this afternoon at an important meeting, he says. But he wanted me to tell you he'll speak to you when he returns if you're awake. And thanks be to God, you are. I will fix you some beef broth and return shortly."

The woman exited the room, and Lydia tried to gather her thoughts. What was the last thing she remembered? Not much, considering the slipping in and out of consciousness.

Before she lost all awareness, there was the sound of a man relieving himself. Lydia had groaned, and the man called out. After that, all had grown dark until she awoke moments ago.

Well, she did have strange dreams, probably fueled by the fever. A man tended her, wiping her forehead, speaking gently. Someone had bathed her.

The man's features remained fuzzy throughout her dreams. Could it be the marquees, or had she imagined it? Or perhaps she'd dreamed of Doctor Damian.

Why on earth would an aristocrat personally see to her care? Bring her to his home? It made no sense.

Lydia never managed to leave London; she remained hidden in the same alley she'd escaped. She admonished herself for running from the underground sanctuary, but what choice did she have?

Well, she could have laid her trust in the nun and the mysterious doctor. But her illness and recent past caused common sense to flee long ago.

A lone tear escaped her eye.

Blast it. Lydia despised being a victim.

Her father raised her to stand tall and take responsibility for her actions. Not run and hide. To be so utterly helpless and dependent on strangers? It was against every grain of her existence.

Her father raised and trained her to be self-sufficient, and before she'd got herself tangled up with John Huntsford, she'd been managing quite nicely.

Weak. Of both mind and constitution.

Because she was lonely and believed she had fallen in love, she gave John money whenever he asked. The wretched man always had a ready and plausible excuse, and she mindlessly accepted his lies. Lydia thought they were building a life together.

Before she knew it, he'd coaxed her to sell most of her possessions and move into his grubby rooms. He speedily devoured her savings. Lydia suspected that in addition to the drugs, Huntsford gambled as well.

Yet, she had stayed.

Hoping that things would turn around, that her love would change him. How many women thought the same thing about a man? She and these other women were not stupid, just naïve and lonely.

Huntsford's true character soon came to light. He had made mistakes at work, which he readily blamed on others—and got away with it. Then he came up with the scheme to rob the pharmacy at St. Thomas—

"Good day, miss."

The marquess stood at the foot of her bed, looking every inch an aristocrat. Lydia never heard the man come into the room.

Her rescuer. Her savior.

The marquess was above average height; she would guess a shade under six feet. His black hair, styled to perfection, reflected the light on shades of brown mixed in. How unique.

Hard to make out the color of his eyes as he stood far enough away, but then her vision was still hazy.

But not enough to see that the marquess was a handsome man.

A wide mouth and a longish nose kept him from complete perfection, but it made his face arresting. There were no long whiskers as many men sported of late but a thin, close-cropped beard.

"Are you able to speak?" His voice was deep but empathetic.

Lydia shook her head.

"You've been here three days. You are welcome to stay as my guest until you're completely recovered. I understand it may take a week or more. Do you?"

She nodded.

"Excellent. You nearly succumbed to the fever, and the bite on your hand has a slight infection. Was it a rat?"

Lydia nodded again, glancing at her wrapped hand. The vile creature had tried to snatch her bread as she nodded off. They had quite a struggle over it until the beast nipped her hand. There was no sleeping peacefully after that.

"The bite has been treated. I do not believe it will turn putrid."

How would he know that? Perhaps a doctor informed him. Did his lordship engage a doctor to treat her? What an extravagance. How could she ever pay him back?

As if reading her mind, he said, "All I ask in return for staying here? When you can converse, I wish you to reveal the facts of your circumstances. Do you promise to tell me the complete truth?"

Frankly, she was weary of lying. Where had it gotten her so far?

There was the chance this marquess would toss her out as soon as he heard her sordid story. Lydia no longer cared.

As long as she could recover first.

One thing at a time.

Closing her eyes, she nodded.

"Excellent. The housekeeper will be along with a bowl of broth. Eat it all, then sleep as long as you like. Good afternoon."

His luxurious voice settled over her like a warm blanket. As Lydia drifted off, she wondered: had she heard the melodic tones before?

HARRISON CROSSED THE threshold of his bedroom to find his valet, Gillis, patiently waiting for him.

"Are you going out tonight, my lord?"

He should venture to the terminus as Miss Best was in no condition for an extended conversation.

"I will be heading to my club after dinner. What is on the menu tonight?"

Gillis stepped forward to remove Harrison's jacket. "Poached salmon in a dill sauce. Roasted carrots. Other assorted well-seasoned root vegetables swimming in a rich sauce, I imagine." His valet replied dryly. "Was your meeting with the Earl of Shaftesbury and the Earl of Carnstone a success, my lord?"

Gillis deftly removed his shirt, then slipped his dressing gown over his shoulders.

"Yes. A complete success."

"Then may I suggest a celebratory brandy and a short nap before dinner? You look weary, my lord."

It was worse than weary. Harrison looked utterly done in. Most peers would not tolerate such forwardness from a valet, but Gillis had been with him since before he came of age. Harrison wondered if Gillis suspected the secret doctor life he led. If so, his valet never commented on it.

"I believe I shall—"

The door opened. "Pardon me, my lord," Youngston announced. "Doctor Kenward requests an audience. Shall I inform him that you are not available?"

So much for his nap.

"No, show him to the study and pour us a couple of brandies. Then we wish to be left alone."

"I shall inform Mrs. Wickes there will be one more for dinner."

His staff was well used to Sam arriving at mealtimes. He kept his dressing gown on and joined Sam in the study ten minutes later. His friend was sitting comfortably before the roaring fire with a brandy snifter.

"Sorry old stick, I couldn't wait. I had to know how the meeting with the earls went. Thank you for the invite to dinner. I could use a good meal, and by the looks of you, so could you."

Harrison sighed, gathered up his snifter, and sat opposite.

"Where have you been the past three days?" Sam asked. "You appear as if you have hardly slept, and you haven't been at the terminus except for an hour here and there—"

Harrison raised a hand to silence his good friend.

"On the night of the ball, I was going to the terminus. I stopped for a call of nature in an alley; and found a young woman in distress."

Sam's eyes widened. "Do not tell me you brought the alley cat here to your home. Why didn't you bring her to the terminus? We could have cared for her there. Harry, bringing home strays is not exactly prudent."

No, it certainly wasn't.

He could have taken her to one of the infirmaries, the workhouse, or to any number of places. The police even. Perhaps he'd grown soft.

Harrison swirled his brandy. "Do you know of someone I could hire, a private investigative type who is discreet and trustworthy?"

"I do, as a matter of fact. William Robins is a retired detective sergeant from this area. He also worked in the East End and is quite familiar with the streets and those who live there. Is it with regards to this young woman?"

"Yes, but first, let me relay the conversation with Shaftesbury and Carnstone. They both expressed a genuine interest in the clinic. They want us to find a suitable location, nothing too large or elaborate, and write up a proposal we can present to a small select group of prospective donors."

Harrison took a sip of brandy. "Carnstone will also involve his son, Aidan Wollstonecraft, Viscount Tensbridge. He is a Member of Parliament for Kent. I will make sure my father and brothers are in attendance. Well, Tremain, at least. I'm sure Spencer will forego such a gathering. It appears I will be coming out of the shadows as you predicted."

"Yes." Sam's brows furrowed. "Nothing too large or elaborate. What do they mean?"

"I asked the earls that exact question. Shaftesbury believes we should start at fifty beds. With room for expansion."

Sam gave a sharp bark of laughter. "We have hundreds at the terminus on any given night."

Harrison sighed as he stared into the depths of his brandy. "Yes, we do. But let us be truthful. It was to be a temporary solution. The cesspits are nearly full. I'm surprised that human waste hasn't spread disease before now. The terminus is a glorified soup kitchen, a shelter offering the thinnest medical care veneer. My plan will be an actual clinic for the truly poor."

"And what of those with nowhere else to go, those who are not ill?" Sam asked. "Do we turn them away as the infirmaries do? Isn't that defeating our purpose of starting our underground shelter?"

A bolt of pain shot through Harrison's head, and he rubbed his temple to dull the throbbing.

"Damn it all. I have run through nearly all my inheritance, Sam. The well is dry. I've no more to give financially for the long-term."

And he was beginning to believe he had no more to give physically or emotionally either. Never in all his thirty-four years had he felt this exhausted.

Sam's eyes widened. "You're destitute?"

"No, not as yet. When my brothers and I came of age, my parents bestowed a fair-sized legacy to each of us to use in any manner we wished. Investments and such. Mad money more than anything. I still have an income from my country estate in Eastbourne, and I'll inherit other properties and money when I become the duke. But in the short term, the money is insufficient to keep the clinic running. I should have invested some of the money; the profit would have allowed the clinic to remain open longer."

Another secret Harrison had kept until tonight: his precarious financial situation. How extravagant of him to gift the town house and its furnishings to his mistress. He could have sold it and used the proceeds to fund the terminus for the rest of the year.

He wanted to ensure Annie had sufficient funds to survive. He was grateful for her friendship and the occasional respite from his exhaustive and secretive life.

What information did he not reveal to Sam?

Harrison may have to give up this town house before the end of the year. This residence was an extravagance he could no longer afford. When in London, he could stay at the Gransford's home in Mayfair. His father would allow it.

Sam absently swirled the brandy. "Invested some of your inheritance? You *have* invested—in hundreds of lives. Nay, thousands. Are you aware of how many people all of us have assisted? Especially you. Your time, your money, your very soul. Not only did you assist with physical maladies, but in allowing those in need to rejoin society. We all offered hope for a better life, but you gave more than any of us. Now *that* is a true legacy."

Damn it, tears welled in his eyes. More proof, he was beyond weary. But he was also touched by the emotionally spoken words.

"A legacy we can all be proud of. The nuns are angels of mercy. This clinic would not have worked without their dedication," Harrison whispered. "And yours."

"I agree." Sam sipped his brandy, his expression showing he was deep in thought. "Could we not propose a clinic-shelter amalgam? Along the lines of what we are running now?"

"We could try. Let us hash it out over the poached salmon. I want to return to this William Robins you spoke of. You see, the woman I found in the alley is the same one I told you of that departed from the terminus."

"When the haughty detective showed up?" Sam placed his empty snifter on the oak table next to him. "What is the woman to you?"

Yes, what?

How could he explain it to Sam when he could not comprehend the wherefores himself?

"I am not sure. I'm compelled to assist Miss Best. There is more to her story." He took a sip of brandy, draining his glass. "I will not deny that I am attracted to her," Harrison murmured. "Before you say anything, I will remain cautious in my dealings with her."

THE MARQUESS OF SECRETS

"You might want to hide the silver," Sam retorted. When Harrison gave him an admonishing look, Sam shook his head. "No, I will not be chastised by your irate glare. You do not *know* this woman or her story. All this could be a ruse to gain entry into your house to rob you blind. Or worse, murder you in your bed."

"May I suggest you cease reading the *Police Gazette* as your imagination has run away with you? Give me some credit for assessing a person's character."

Sam shrugged. "Well, you're in the market for a new mistress, are you not?"

Harrison shot to his feet, his free hand clenched into a fist.

"Ah," Sam said in a soft voice. "As I suspected. You *are* interested in her beyond the surface attraction." Sam looked up and caught his gaze. "Assist her by all means, but remain vigilant. I would not see you hurt for the world."

Harrison's breathing calmed.

Interested beyond the surface attraction.

Should he fight it? Stubbornly continue to search for a young lady among the peerage?

Never felt all at sea like this before.

It worried him—and exhilarated him beyond all imagining.

Chapter 10

LYDIA HAD BARELY SEEN the marquess the past two days. Granted, she spent most of the time sleeping. He could have looked in on her then. Today she was determined to sit upright. Although it took effort, she sat up straight when Mrs. Wickes entered with a tray.

"Good for you, my girl." She placed the tray on the bed and plumped the pillows behind Lydia. "I've brought something a little more appetizing than beef broth." Picking up the tray, she then laid it on Lydia's lap. "Oatmeal. Brown sugar to sweeten it. Two pieces of toast along with fresh honey. Hot tea. If you eat this, we can try cold meat and assorted cheeses for teatime. Perhaps a scone." Mrs. Wickes turned to leave.

"Wait, Mrs. Wickes. Can you stay for a moment?"

The older woman nodded briskly. "I can spare you but a few." She sat in the chair next to the bed. "Eat up, my girl."

"Does the marquess habitually bring strangers into his house?" Lydia immediately drizzled a teaspoon of the golden honey on a piece of toast and took a bite. Heavenly.

Mrs. Wickes frowned. "Here now. His lordship is not in the habit of picking up young ladies from the street and bringing them to his town house for immoral purposes. Get that right out of your mind. The marquess is a generous master. He does have rakish ways, but why wouldn't he, unattached and handsome as he is?"

Lydia breathed a sigh of relief as she took another bite of toast. She assumed he would require payment of the physical sort for his generosity.

When did any man of the peerage do anything out of the kindness of his heart? What did she know of the upper classes except what she read in books or newspapers? Or the salacious gossip she overheard at the hospital?

"Did someone bathe me the first night I was here?" Lydia sipped her tea, keeping her gaze locked on the housekeeper, watching for any change in her expression.

"You were suffering from a terrible fever. You floated in and out of consciousness, babbling words that made no sense. His lordship insisted you be placed in a cool bath to reduce your temperature. You did call for your papa at one point."

Tears gathered on Lydia's lashes at the mention of her dear father. "He died five years ago."

"I'm that sorry, lass."

She gave Mrs. Wickes a shaky smile. "Thank you for everything. You've been kind, as has his lordship. And the maid who comes in to keep the fire going."

"You have a touch of quality about you. I saw that right off. Not a true street waif at all."

Lydia took a sip of tea. "I'm not. Never did I think it would come to this." She shook her head as if to dismiss the past several months. If only she could.

"Regarding the bath, was the marquess in the room? I remember seeing a man's face though I couldn't make it out."

A small smile curved about the housekeeper's mouth. "Well, he was. He was that concerned. Don't look panicked; I kept your threadbare chemise on the entire time he was in the room. After he stepped out, I removed it and washed you all over. As I told you earlier, everything had to be burned. You have flea bites on your torso. The doctor treated them."

"So a doctor did see me? Will he return?"

Mrs. Wickes stood, straightening her apron. "You best take that up with his lordship. Eat up, girl. I'll return later for the tray."

The woman bustled out of the room.

The marquess? Concerned about her? He'd been in the room when she was all but naked?

It's not as if she were an innocent virgin. But still, how strange.

Why would a peer be interested or concerned about her care? It made no sense. Why even take her in? Lydia couldn't puzzle it out this minute, for her head ached. And he called a doctor for her? How generous.

Eating leisurely, Lydia glanced about the room—a fair size and in a feminine style, from the brass bed to the flower-patterned wallpaper to the white wood furniture and light rose-colored drapes. With the fire going, it made the room cozy.

Against the opposite wall was a lovely vanity. Lydia sighed. She'd always longed for one, so she could sit in front of the mirror, powdering her nose and applying a touch of scent behind her ears. They were the hopeful dreams of an idealistic young girl with her entire future ahead of her. Now all of it was dashed and smashed beyond recognition.

A knock sounded at the partly open door as she ate her toast.

"May I come in?"

Lydia's heart skittered in her chest at his masculine tone. Blast it all, for she shouldn't be reacting to him.

"Yes, my lord."

The marquess stepped into the room but stayed near the entrance. "You're sitting upright. Excellent."

He turned toward the window. Standing in front of it, he clasped his hands behind him. All Lydia could see was a partial profile of his face.

"What is your name?" he asked, his voice soft. "The truth, if you please."

"My name is Miss Lydia Chesterton, my lord."

His lordship's shoulders straightened. Perhaps Lydia imagined it, for how could he know of her name?

Several minutes passed. Lydia pushed the tray off her lap, and the china clinked together.

"How long were you living on the streets?" he asked.

"On and off for close to two weeks. I ran out of money and could no longer afford a rented room—a precarious situation. I could not even afford a dosshouse, my lord. I had no choice but to seek shelter in various alleys."

"Do you have secrets, Miss Chesterton?"

Lydia squirmed uncomfortably and pulled the quilt to her shoulders as a chill moved through her. "Yes. I suppose most people do, my lord."

The marquess walked back and forth, his head down. Then he stopped in front of the window again. "I do as well. I would not expect you to reveal secrets without revealing some of my own. Would you be amenable to an exchange of such intimacies?"

Good God.

He *did* want her to repay him in a physical sense. How on earth could she be horrified and intrigued all at the same time?

Because, Lydia, you are wicked. To the very core.

The marquess turned toward her. "Secrets only, Miss Chesterton. Do not distress yourself."

She could not see his face, for the early afternoon sun blurred his features. It was as if a heavenly halo of illumination surrounded him.

"Why did you bring me here, my lord? You could have walked away and left me to the fates. Many would have."

Her voice was shaky, and it revealed her susceptibility. Oh, how she hated feeling vulnerable, but how could she not? Not exactly what she wished to do in this circumstance.

"I believed you would receive better care here than at a hospital. Many infirmaries would have turned you away. If not at once, then after I'd left you there."

Lydia knew the truth of the statement well enough. She'd seen it occur at St. Thomas. The hospital took in a smattering of charity cases, but they turned away more than they treated.

How could the marquess know of this? It seemed to her that an aristocrat would hardly care about those beneath him.

"Then, I'm grateful, my lord."

A coughing fit overtook her, but she collected herself and wiped her mouth with the napkin from the tray.

He took a step or two toward her, then halted.

"Mrs. Wickes said a doctor treated me when I first arrived," Lydia said.

"Hmm. Yes."

"Will he return, my lord?"

"I'm keeping the doctor informed of your condition. I'll recall him if you should take a turn for the worse. Meanwhile, you appear to be recovering well enough."

"Of course. Thank you, my lord."

Lydia could not ascertain his emotions. He spoke with the detached air she imagined all aristocrats used. Why she hoped for any warmth was beyond her.

"Considering your homeless state, is there no one you can turn to in your hour of need?" he asked.

Lydia clasped her hands to keep them from shaking. "There is no one, my lord."

He took a step toward her. "No man in your life? A suitor?"

"Not any longer. He's out of my life. I hope."

The marquess moved closer, his movements reminding her of a jungle cat she'd seen at a circus years before. A sleek animal stalking his prey. Her heart skipped a beat, but not in fear.

"It was not a mutually beneficial relationship then?" he asked, his voice husky.

"No, my lord. Not in any way. I would categorize it as unhealthy."

"You agree to the exchange of secrets?"

She gulped. "Yes."

He sat by her bed, and his wonderful spicy scent filled her senses, making her slightly dizzy.

"Then allow me to reveal first. Until recently, I kept a mistress. Set her up in a fancy town house for more than three years. It was a ruse." He crossed his long legs. "Oh, I visited her occasionally, but on the whole, she supplied a ready excuse for my many absences."

Did he expect her to react?

Indeed, he wasn't proposing she steps in as his mistress?

Lydia waited and kept looking straight ahead. Since escaping from John Huntsford, her frayed nerves sparked with awareness. The marquess sitting so near made her anxious. Not for her safety but certainly for her peace of mind.

Why was she reacting to this man?

Lydia was well aware of the varied physical reactions of attraction: the tumbling insides, the rush of excitement, the accelerated heartbeat. She was experiencing all of these.

Not wise. Not at all.

"Did I haunt opium dens?" he continued. "Brothels? Gambling houses? No, those vices of the upper classes bored me in my early twenties. I indulged a few times, enough to give me a reputation. I decided to use the reputation as a cover. I even kept my secret life from my family." He crossed his arms. "Your turn, Miss Chesterton. *Quid pro quo.*"

Why did he leave his story there? Frustrating man.

"Do you know what that means?" he asked kindly.

At least his tone was not condescending.

"I do. My father was a schoolmaster. I understand a little Latin. It means 'this for that.' I will return the exchange."

"Did your father also teach you Greek? I ask because within your bundle was a copy of *Republic* by Plato. It must be a prized possession if you hauled it about London with you."

"Yes, my late father taught me many things. Greek included. It's a prized possession because it was his. My father tried to instill common sense along with his lessons. It did not take. I became involved with a man that has ruined my life."

Lydia sighed. "But the fault does not all lie with him. The signs were there for me to read. I chose to ignore them. Because when my father died, I was left alone. I did not *want* to be alone. As a result, I gave all my love and attention to a man who did not deserve it."

The marquess stood, and out of the corner of her eye, she watched as he pulled his gold watch from his waistcoat pocket and opened it. He then snapped it shut and returned it to his pocket.

"Unfortunately, I am expected at Westminster today. I've plans tonight and will not return until late. We will continue this conversation tomorrow."

His spicy scent contained a hint of cloves. Lydia had always liked that scent. She must be feeling better if she could make out certain smells.

"But you're not going to a brothel or gambling den as some would believe. Are you, my lord?"

"No. I'm not."

Lydia met his gaze. Staring back at her were the most mesmerizing silver-gray eyes fanned by incredibly long lashes, the same shade of dark brownish-black as his hair.

He gave her a slight bow. "I bid you good afternoon, Miss Chesterton."

The marquess left the room.

It hit her. The revelation was so startling that she gasped.

Lydia had seen those eyes before— the same penetrating gaze.

The voice was similar now that she thought about it.

She understood where the marquess was going and why he didn't need to bring the doctor to see her medical care.

The Marquess of Tennington was—Doctor Damian.

Chapter 11

HARRISON HADN'T BOTHERED setting up a carriage and horses of his own. Most days, he caught a hansom cab because time was of the essence. The distance between his town house on Marylebone Road and Westminster Abbey was slightly over three miles.

Sometimes he borrowed his mistress's and briefly did consider taking them for his own once he settled the accounts. Despite his precarious financial position, he decided to gift her with the lot. Annie deserved it.

He could reach the Parliament buildings in thirteen minutes if he kept a brisk pace. It would give him adequate time to clear his mind and regain control.

Sitting close and speaking intimately with Miss Chesterton—Lydia—aroused him.

What a surprising reaction, but not entirely unwelcome.

What pleased him was that she'd passed the test.

Harrison decided that if she gave him her correct name, he would propose the "exchange of secrets" to learn her story. Perhaps he wanted her to know him better as well.

If she stuck with the "Miss Best" name, he would have seen that she recovered, assisted her in finding a job and lodgings, and continued with his life and pursuit of a suitable bride. He stubbornly held to the belief that he must marry as is expected of him as the heir.

But that particular goal held less appeal or urgency than before.

What in God's name was he doing?

Tremain told him he initially had doubts about Eliza concerning their different societal places and how society would look upon them. But his brother had soon dismissed such thoughts.

It was disconcerting, to say the least. And blasted pretentious.

Harrison, of all people, should not be despairing about her social status. People were worth more than their birthright. Harrison had seen the proof every night at the terminus—the quiet dignity and courage in the face of despair.

They were worth all of Westminster.

Harrison crossed the road onto New Bond Street and passed the many luxurious shops filling the lane. His parents' residence was nearby, and his mother loved to haunt the various mercantile offerings on a sunny day. His parents were currently at the estate in Hastings as his father was dealing with a minor health issue, a murmur of the heart Harrison had detected.

What an extravagance to have two town houses within a few miles of each other in this day and age. Many in the aristocracy experienced diminished monetary superiority, selling off anything not entailed. The luxurious life of leisure of the Regency era was long past. As was the unbridled wealth.

Harrison again considered renting or selling his, using the money for the clinic.

So many problems with no conclusion in sight.

His attention returned to his lovely houseguest. What did he want from her? All he knew was that no woman had stirred such myriad emotions before, such as tenderness and the overwhelming desire to protect her. Desire itself in all its complicated and stimulating manifestations. His nightly dreams were proof of how he wanted her. Though undernourished and recovering from pneumonia, her beauty was apparent.

But what held his interest was the fact that she was a nurse.

What better companion for a man of medicine? Someone who would understand his commitment, his deep-seated necessity to assist those in dire straits?

Harrison harbored fantasies of them working side-by-side at the new clinic.

Damn his title and inheritance. It had denied him the life he truly wished to live.

It would also deny him the woman he wanted and desired.

Scowling, he picked up the pace.

Easy, man.

Harrison was not used to this, as he prided himself on keeping his emotions under wraps and well-protected. He may have acted too detached when speaking with Lydia. His feelings were caught up in a cyclone, whirling about, causing his heart and soul to turn to the wreckage.

God forbid he should reveal what he was feeling.

Whatever it was.

Dodging carriages and piles of horse manure, Harrison made his way to the side entrance and entered the hall but stopped short when he spotted his brother, Tremain, leaning on his cane, admiring the recently installed frescos.

"Tremain!"

Harrison hurried toward his younger brother. Then, seeing they were alone, he embraced him briefly.

"Steady on. We just saw each other a couple of weeks ago," Tremain laughed.

Public displays of affection were generally frowned upon, but Harrison didn't care as he was genuinely pleased to see his brother.

After returning from the war, Tremain had not been himself. Harrison worried the brother he knew, loved, and admired was gone forever.

How gratifying to have him back.

Upon his return from South Africa, Tremain was made Viscount Hawkestone. It was an extinct title on their mother's side, going back more than one hundred years. The queen wished to reward Tremain for his services to the crown by resurrecting the title through letters patent. Many grumbled over the blatant favoritism the queen had often shown his family, but in Harrison's eyes, his brother more than deserved such a rare honor.

"Nonetheless, it's good to see you. When did you arrive in London?" Harrison asked.

"Just this morning. I'm staying at the Gransford town house. Father said I should make an appearance at Parliament. It is well overdue." He clapped Harrison on the shoulder. "You have been carrying far more of the burden here at the House of Lords since Father's health crisis. It's far past time I contributed and fulfilled my obligations."

"And Eliza?"

A warm smile curved about Tremain's mouth at the mention of his fiancée's name.

"As propriety dictates, she stays with our mother and father until the wedding. Drew is also there, being tutored by Eliza and spoiled shamelessly by his new grandparents."

Tremain had taken in a young orphan from the village that was part of his brother's estate. Harrison immediately liked the lad, especially when Drew mentioned his interest in pursuing a medical career. Once Harrison revealed his secrets to his family, he would do all he could to assist the boy.

"And Spence?"

"When has our younger brother ever given a toss about society and propriety? Since he brought her from Wales in January, he is tucked away at Penhaven with Philomena and his wolfhounds."

They moved to the nearby corner to have a more private conversation.

Tremain rested against the wall, exhaling in pain as he shifted his weight from his cane. Harrison should not leave him standing like this for long.

"He adamantly refused to be parted from her when Father suggested it," Tremain revealed. "Became quite agitated. The family decided to let the matter drop. Spence's place is more or less isolated. He does not venture into society, so who's to know?"

The corner of Harrison's mouth twitched. Obviously, his brother hadn't heard the tattle on Spence, and be damned if he would share it here.

Big Ben chimed at the top of the hour.

"We'd best head to chambers," Harrison said. "We can take tea on the terrace afterward if you like."

"Sitting with other lords and members? Not much chance for a private conversation there. I was going to seek you out anyway, and I've already informed the staff that you would be joining me for dinner. I insist. You do not have any other plans this evening?"

Damnation.

Harrison had hoped to take dinner with Lydia before venturing to the terminus. His hesitation caused Tremain to arch an eyebrow.

"Off to the mistress tonight?" his brother asked.

Harrison shook his head. "I no longer have a mistress."

"All the more reason you must join me for dinner to divulge the details. Come, time for you to show me the ropes."

The brothers headed toward the Lord's chambers.

Harrison wondered: how much to reveal to Tremain?

Chapter 12

THE MEAL WAS FLAWLESS. The staff served a sinfully rich cream of asparagus soup, lettuce, and tomato salad, followed by a fillet of beef with mushroom sauce, roasted potatoes, and creamed peas. Harrison did not stand on ceremony; he ate everything.

Now the brothers were alone with a platter of fruit and cheese and a bottle of port. Harrison told his brother about parting with his mistress and his determined search for a suitable bride.

Although he reflected, he was not as committed as a couple of weeks ago.

Tremain's brows furrowed. "Harry, are you being pressured by our esteemed parents to make a match from the peerage?"

"Well, no. Our parents would never make such a declaration. But you must remember when we were youths, there were many days Father sequestered me away to learn the duties of a duke. I took the lessons to heart. They made a permanent impact. Father pressed upon me the importance of our family: the history, the responsibilities for the tenants, and all in our care. Including our younger brother."

Harrison swirled the port in his glass, then took a sip. "It was much to take in, but I embraced the obligation wholeheartedly. Regardless of you and Spencer finding it, I've all but given up on love. Finding a suitable bride would fulfill my commitment to the family and the lineage." He paused. "However, fate rarely takes such things into consideration."

"What are you talking about?"

"There is a woman. I met her under the circumstances much as your own."

He gave Tremain a brief, condensed version of his and Lydia's meeting, leaving out his suspicions of her homeless state and the terminus.

Tremain leaned back, his expression incredulous. "We are a strange set of siblings; there is no mistake. We certainly do not follow what is expected of us by society. How long do you intend to keep her at your town house?"

"No admonishments for taking in a stranger?" Harrison smiled.

"Not from me, for I did the same. You will be able to tell soon enough if Miss Chesterton is trustworthy. So, how long will she be staying?"

"Until she is recovered—and until I get to know her better. Until I find if these strange sensations and emotions are something I should dismiss or embrace fully."

Tremain leaned forward and laid grapes and cheese on his plate. Then he poured them more port.

"My advice? To hell with duty and responsibilities. This is your life. If you're developing feelings for the young woman, do not discharge them. Explore and nurture them. Love is everything, Brother. Spence would say the same. I had not realized my empty life until I met Eliza. Yes, I did good works, and it gave me peace, but loving Eliza brings everything full circle. Completes me, so to speak."

Tremain had the right of it. Good works were all well and good, but it was not the total of a man's life.

There must be more.

He would be a fool to ignore what was happening inside him. But the bigger question is, would Miss Chesterton return any feelings? Wasn't this all developing too quickly?

Not according to his brothers.

Popping a couple of grapes in his mouth, Tremain chewed thoughtfully, then swallowed. "Follow your heart," Tremain continued. "I tried to ignore what was happening, believing myself too damaged to love a woman. I was mistaken. Do not turn from love for the sake of duty. Our parents would never forgive you." A slight smile curved about his brother's mouth. "And neither would Spencer. Or I, for that matter."

Tremain's words touched him. "I will think about what you said. I'm not sure if the young lady even returns my regard. This strange feeling may be a mere infatuation on my part. Love cannot develop as quickly as you say. Surely not."

Tremain arched an eyebrow. "Oh? Tell Spence that, and he will vehemently disagree. For him, it was a week. For me? Merely a few weeks. There is no set schedule. Perhaps what you're feeling isn't love at all. All I am saying is to give it a chance. If you walk away, you will regret it for the rest of your days. Be open to new experiences."

Harrison smiled. "When did you become so blasted wise?"

"War brings much into perspective. The one lesson I learned is that life is short. I no longer take anything for granted. Remember how wicked we were in our early twenties?" Tremain winked. "Complete rouges."

Harrison chuckled, then sobered.

The decadent doings had soon lost their appeal. They cut quite a swath in London society for eighteen months before Tremain took up his commission. One whiskey and opium-soaked night, they had shared an expensive courtesan. The sex with the hired woman was frantic and feral, leaving him empty and ashamed.

Hungover and nauseous by morning, he and Tremain paid the woman and never spoke of it again. But they could not meet each other's gaze for several days after the encounter. They had never spoken of it.

Until now.

"It's a part of my past I would rather forget." Harrison exhaled. "And regardless of the gossip, I have not engaged in any excesses since."

Tremain threw back the rest of his port. "Neither have I. I had a few brief dalliances between campaigns, but nothing to compare with—well, best forgotten. Older and wiser and all that rot. We all have our demons, and they manifest in strange ways."

If Tremain only knew.

"Do you regret keeping your identity secret?" Harrison asked, his tone soft. "Did you ever think yourself a coward for hiding behind a false character, even though you were doing good work? I mean, you trained to be a vicar. I'm talking of the fictitious name and background."

Tremain raised an eyebrow. "Coward?"

"Easy, Brother. I'm not saying you *are* one, merely asking if you ever thought yourself one?"

Tremain poured more port into his tumbler. He waved it toward Harrison, but he shook his head.

"An interesting question. Yes, it crossed my mind more than once. I also dealt with the guilt over my selfishness. But I eventually concluded it was my life, and I would make my own choices, damn the consequences. The hard truth of it? I was in no way ready to step into my role as viscount. I never asked for the honor, never wanted it, but how can you refuse the queen?"

Tremain's expression turned reflective. "So I created another persona—a place where I felt safe, free from the encumbrances of society and our family's expectations. And our parents have them even though they do not beat us about the head with them—they are there. Hence your dogged obligation regarding the title."

Harrison nodded. The expectations were there; how could they not be? Their father was a duke. Their mother is the daughter of an earl. Blue blood could be traced back generations.

Duty. Honor. Expectations.

"It also gave me time to heal," Tremain continued, "not only physically but mentally and emotionally. I was a complete wreck."

Harrison nodded again. "Understandable. But what about an individual who was not involved in a horrid war? What would be his impetus for such an undertaking?"

Tremain scratched his chin. "Without knowing the particulars, I would hazard to guess self-preservation—and the protection of others or a combination of both. In my mind, it's not cowardly but cautious. Prudent. Sensible."

"I've something important to discuss with you, Spence, and Father once we meet at the estate. And Mother, too, for that matter."

"Oh? Don't care to give me a hint?"

"It may change the family's opinion of me, one way or the other. I will reveal what I have been up to for several years. It's time to come clean."

Tremain crossed his arms. "This secret life you spoke of is your own? Sounds ominous. You are not going to reveal something along the line of being a spy for the crown?"

Harrison placed his empty glass on the table. "Not as romantic, but perhaps as noble. At least in my eyes. Or perhaps I have an inflated view of my importance."

"My God, we are a strange lot," Tremain mused. "The three most eccentric chaps ever to breathe air. Come now, give me a hint?"

He and his brothers were undoubtedly distinct from other peers, to be sure.

"Later."

"You are full of secrets."

Harrison gave a short bark of laughter. "Yes, it appears I am."

"When are you heading to Gransford Manor?" Tremain asked. "I'll be heading there in two weeks."

"I imagine a couple of days before the weddings."

"Then I suppose you will not be traveling with me. I'll be making the journey by train."

"No, I've obligations to see to before I depart."

Yes. There were many obligations.

Including the lovely lady recovering in his guestroom.

The lovely lady who never left his thoughts

Chapter 13

THE PENDULUM CLOCK on the wall chimed eleven, and Lydia was still wide awake. Earlier in the evening, Mrs. Wickes informed her Lord Tennington would not be home until late as he would join his brother for dinner, then off to his club.

Right.

Off to the underground terminus more like.

It had to be him—Doctor Damian.

Few people possessed eyes of such a remarkable shade. The voice was similar, as well as the build. Should she divulge her discovery or see if this is one of the secrets he means to reveal?

The marquess's claim of fueling his wicked reputation to cover for his medical charity fit.

Why would a man—and heir to a duke—give his time and energy to such a thankless endeavor? Since when did aristocrats study medicine? None that she was aware of. But he must have in some capacity.

The marquess must know her true identity, for he had heard the tale from the police detective. She fit the physical description. Regardless, Lydia had already decided to tell Lord Tennington the truth about her situation. She would reveal it all, no matter how mortifying. No more running and hiding.

Perhaps his lordship might assist her. Or he could turn her out onto the cobbles. Either scenario was possible.

The door opened and gave Lydia a start, causing her to gasp loudly.

"Sorry to startle you. Still awake?" The marquess paused. "You are. I just wanted to see if you are well. Comfortable. Have you had enough to eat?"

"Yes, my lord. Your staff has been very attentive. And kind."

Illumination from a gaslight in the hall cast him in shadow; his profile loomed in the doorway. He hesitated as if he did not know what to do or say next. Finally, he turned to leave.

"Wait! I'm not tired if you wish to continue our conversation this afternoon. I wouldn't mind." Lydia gave him a shaky smile as if he could see it in the dark.

He didn't reply right away, as if mulling over the suggestion. "I will stay for a few minutes. I will light the wall sconce. Is that sufficient?"

"Yes, my lord."

He moved to the opposite wall, and the hiss of gas filled her hearing. Muted lighting flooded the room. She scrambled to sit upright as he sat in the chair beside her bed, ensuring the blankets covered her modesty. Lydia wore a nightgown borrowed from one of the maids.

Again, as if reading her thoughts, he declared, "We will see you properly attired. I'm sure Mrs. Wickes informed you that we had to burn your clothes, even the ones in the bundle. I am sorry."

"But you've done so much for me already," Lydia murmured.

"I have access to second-hand garments. I can bring various pieces for you to try on. They will do it in the interim until we make more permanent plans."

"Thank you, my lord."

"Can we dispense with the title while we are alone? It would make the conversation more palatable to me. My name is Harrison...Lydia."

Harrison. The name fit.

Elegant and formal, yet with a certain warmth. Did the marquess go by Harry, she wondered? That name also fit him.

"Of course, Harrison."

"When we last spoke, you claimed you gave affection to a man who didn't deserve it. In what way?" His voice was soft and empathetic.

"We met at my place of employment. I was a nurse at St. Thomas Hospital. John Huntsford was a surgeon. At first, he was all that was charming. Fraternization is frowned upon between the staff, so we kept our relationship secret. Soon we were meeting after work in places far from our residences or the hospital. Before I knew it, I'd fallen for him and moved into his flat. Are you shocked?"

"At what? You moving into his residence. Should I be?"

"Young ladies are not supposed to cohabit with men unless married. Or so society says."

"Society has far too much to say about someone's personal business. You wanted a future with this Huntsford."

"Yes, I thought we had at least a chance at a future together. Little did I know of his true character. Your turn."

He folded his arms across his chest. "Ah. Where did I leave off?"

"You stated you have a secret life. I believe I can guess what it is." She gave the marquess a shy but knowing smile.

Harrison chuckled. "Please do."

"At my lowest point, shivering and starving in an alley, I made my way to a place I had heard about a temporary respite from living on the cobbles. I encountered a man dressed in white, completely covered except for his mesmerizing silver-gray eyes. Doctor Damian. Toiling underground, treating the poor, and giving his valuable time and talent. A medical Robin Hood."

A slight smile curved about his mouth. "I've never heard it put quite like that, but I suppose it has a thread of truth."

"It's you, isn't it?" Lydia stated, her voice soft with admiration.

"Yes. I'm a trained physician. I have degrees from Cambridge but cannot practice due to societal rules. I practice medicine on my terms and have for many years. In secret."

Lydia's heart swelled with approval. When had she ever heard of a member of the peerage giving so much with no recognition?

"I respect what you're doing. It used to tear my heart to shreds to see people turned away at St. Thomas. People who couldn't pay but who needed our care the most."

Harrison nodded. "The very reason I started this secret charity. My good friend, Doctor Samuel Kenward, and the nuns, all do their part. Sacrificing their time, energy, and perhaps a piece of their souls. Your turn. Little did you know of Huntsford's character? Will you elaborate?"

It caused her insides to twist to speak of it, but she told him of moving in with John and lending him money until he depleted her small savings. With a shaky sigh, she continued.

"I found out he'd been spending my money on opium. He introduced it to me one night w-w-when we were having relations." Lydia flushed; the last word ended in a whisper. "This is hard for me to talk about. What you must think of me."

Harrison gently clasped her elbow and pushed up the sleeve of the flannel nightgown. The tips of his fingers caressed the scars on her arm. Her heart fluttered rapidly at his warm and caring touch.

"He did more than introduce you. He forced the needle in against your will, tearing your skin. Am I correct?"

Though she tried hard not to react, tears filled her eyes regardless. Lydia nodded, biting her lower lip. "He said it would enhance the experience."

Uttering a foul oath under his breath, Harrison lifted her arm and softly kissed the scars.

Oh. Oh, my.

His mouth was warm, and his touch exhilarating. Lydia's insides melted at his compassionate kiss. He released her arm with tender care and laid it across her waist.

"The man is a monster for maiming you in such a way. What he did was a violation." Harrison brushed away the couple of tears that had trailed down her flushed cheek.

Yes. That was the harsh truth of it.

An assault. A violation.

It was the reason she made such a hasty departure.

"I do not wish to upset you further tonight. All I ask is this: are you guilty of what the police detective claims? We will discuss the details tomorrow."

"No, I'm not. I adamantly refused to participate in Huntsford's twisted plan. It's part of the reason I ran—"

Harrison laid a finger against her lips. "No more tonight."

He stared at her with those beautiful eyes filled with emotions she could not guess. His thumb brushed across her lips, gently stroking, inflaming her body clear to her toes.

Lydia laid her hand on top of his and turned until her mouth met his palm.

She kissed it. Once. Twice. A third time.

A husky groan left Harrison's throat, causing her heart to pound faster. His sensual reaction to her kiss had her longing to crawl into his lap and hold him tight. This generous man caused all her troubles to fade into nothingness.

He stood and backed away from her to the opposite wall. As he turned down the gas, darkness swallowed him whole.

"Sleep, Lydia. We will continue this discussion tomorrow."

The door handle gave a soft, snick sound as he closed the door behind him.

His scent lingered.

Her skin still throbbed where he'd touched her. Her lips tingled from kissing his warm palm.

Lydia wanted more. Oh, so much more.

At the lowest point of her life, sick as she was, she should not be experiencing such intense emotions.

She had no business craving an heir to a duke.

HARRISON HURRIED TOWARD The Red Lion pub for a luncheon meeting with Sam and his investigator acquaintance, William Robins.

The public house near Parliament was a favorite for members and lords, and even "The Grand Old Man" himself, Prime Minister Gladstone, frequented the place.

The scent of beef and onions inundated his senses, along with the odors of beer and tobacco. The oak bar with stained glass panels took up the entire side of the room. The place was crowded and boisterous, and Harrison scanned the area until he located Sam waving him to the far corner booth.

Harrison nodded to the men as he slipped across the green leather bench.

"I took the liberty of ordering you a pint of bitter," Sam said. "William Robins, this is my close friend, Harrison Hornsby, the Marquess of Tennington. Harry, William."

Robins held out his hand, and Harrison took it, giving it a firm shake. William Robins looked like a copper; his no-nonsense aura hinted at danger. He was far taller than he and Sam, close to six and a half feet at least. His wavy hair sported many threads of gray mixed in with the light brown shade. His dark brown eyes held a steely, intelligent glare as he assessed his surroundings and gave Harrison a thorough inspection.

The barmaid delivered their beers and took their orders for the meat pies before moving to other tables.

"Samuel mentioned you wish me to check on a woman in your care, my lord."

Well, William Robins did not beat about the bush. Harrison gave a quick synopsis of Lydia's predicament. The investigator pulled a small pad and the nub of a pencil from his side coat pocket, jotting notes as Harrison relayed the facts.

"Do you believe this woman regarding her narrative, my lord?" Robins asked.

Did he?

The barmaid arrived with the pies, giving Harrison a respite from an immediate reply. His thoughts drifted to last night and the shared intimacy between them. When she kissed his palm, his heart swelled to bursting. But he could not be carried away on a wave of intense emotions, even ones he'd never experienced with any other woman.

But God, it shook him to his core.

How tempting to pull her close and kiss her.

Thoroughly. Savagely.

If Lydia continued to stay at the town house, eventually, it would happen as the air fairly crackled between them. But it couldn't occur, for he would not take advantage of a woman in such a dreadful predicament.

"There's no mistaking I found her in extreme straits, and there is physical evidence of her mistreatment. She wouldn't misrepresent her former occupation since it is easy to check." In a firm voice, he paused and said, "Yes, I believe her."

"What was the detective's name who came to the underground shelter, my lord?" Robins asked with pencil poised.

"Detective Constable Willis from G Division. Stated many divisions were investigating this pharmacy theft," Harrison replied.

Robins grunted. "Coppers pretty much stick to their boroughs. We can be a territorial lot, my lord. It sounds as if he is investigating this independently, which means someone hired him off the books to find the nurse. She may not even be a suspect."

Robins scribbled more notes. "Willis. I've heard of him. A weaselly, oily character. Leave it with me. I will get to the bottom of it. Now, gentlemen, we should partake of our pies before they cool."

The men started to eat, and the conversation turned to mundane subjects, the weather, the dismal, wet spring, how it could carry over into summer and have decided ramifications on certain crops. Robins also proved to be up-to-date on current events like the new "bridge across the Thames" proposal to accommodate the swelling London population.

Downing the last of his pint of bitter and wiping his mouth on the napkin, Robins then reached for his hat.

"I'll be off then, gentlemen. I wish to get started right away."

"And your fee?" Harrison asked.

"Let us say ten pounds to start the investigation. Business is brisk, and I have hired two younger men, also ex-coppers. With their assistance, we should have news for you in a matter of days, my lord."

Good thing Harrison brought extra money with him. He slid pound notes across the table, and Robins swiftly snatched them up and tucked them away in his side coat pocket. The older man stood, reaching for a cane he must have had resting next to him on the bench seat.

"I will contact Samuel when I have news?"

Harrison nodded. "Yes. We will set up another meeting such as this. Lunch is on me."

Robins touched his forelock, giving a brief, sly smile. "I assumed it would be. Good day, my lord. Samuel."

The man limped off and exited the pub.

"He's a good man," Sam said.

"How did he obtain the limp?"

"From a bullet in the leg during a confrontation with thieves in a rookery. I treated him; it's how we met. Unfortunately, the injury prematurely ended his career with the Metropolitan Police. Mind you, I do not believe he would complain. He confided in me that he's making more money than he ever had as a copper."

Sam cut into the last of his pie. "If anyone can ascertain information in a timely matter, it's William." He popped a forkful in his mouth and swallowed. "So, your house guest is a nurse? There is a certain symmetry to that."

Yes. It's as if fate pushed the woman into his path. There he was, thinking of chance again. This morning he awoke early, visited the terminus, and tended to several patients. Then he dropped off a bundle of used garments with his housekeeper for Lydia to try on before heading to The Red Lion.

Again, his thoughts drifted to the previous night and their heated awareness.

Why not explore the attraction?

If nothing came of it, he would continue his search for a bride without losing a stride in his step. Tremain's words echoed in his mind like a benediction.

"All I am saying is give it a chance. If you walk away, you will regret it for the rest of your days. Be open to new experiences."

Give it a chance.

Yes, why not?

If Lydia was receptive to his attentions. Perhaps not, seeing she was in a desperate situation while recovering from a severe illness. The way she kissed his palm bespoke of a passionate woman. And a lonely one.

Harrison recognized loneliness all too well, for he suffered from it, too. Loneliness: a disorder that overpowered even the laughter and company a pub like this offered. Loneliness. Would this ailment for which he had no cure ever leave him? Glumly, he tossed back the last of his bitter and thought again, give it a chance.

What could it hurt?
Just everything he had planned for years.
And it could hurt his vulnerable heart.

Chapter 14

LYDIA SPENT THE AFTERNOON trying on the clothes Harrison had dropped by. The pile consisted of used wool skirts and white blouses, but the garments were clean and tidy. They are a little large, but they would serve the purpose. The clothes included petticoats, three chemises, and one corset.

She was exhausted when she'd tried on everything and selected the ones that fit.

One of the maids brought afternoon tea, and Lydia climbed into bed and accepted the tray. After drinking her tea and eating the biscuits and fruit, she napped. Oh, how she could get used to this.

A maid woke her at seven, stating the marquess awaited her presence in the dining room.

Rubbing her eyes, she sat upright. Dining room? A different maid, Mariah, assisted her in dressing and fixing her hair into an upswept style. Then Mariah led her down two sets of stairs.

Lydia stood before a tall man in a double-breasted black coat and white tie.

"I am Youngston, his lordship's under-butler. Will you follow me, Miss Best?"

Harrison hadn't informed the servants of her real name. Thank goodness. Their exchange of secrets would remain between them, and she was silently relieved.

Youngston opened the double doors, and the coziness immediately took her despite the size of the room. A fire blazed in the white marble hearth. Burgundy and gold gilded wallpaper adorned the walls, and ornate floral drapes covered most of one wall, the colors matching the wallpaper. A long table with high-back chairs sat in the middle of the room. Overhead the chandelier blazed, washing the room in muted illumination.

The room was glorious.

Harrison stood and smiled.

"Miss Best, your lordship," Youngston announced.

"Thank you, Youngston. You may commence serving."

Harrison came to her side and tucked her hand through the crook of his arm.

"May I escort you to your seat?"

Goodness, the table sat at least twelve.

"Will I be sitting close enough so we can converse?"

He patted her hand. "Most assuredly."

Harrison pulled out a chair, and she sat. He took the one next to her at the head of the table.

"Not a formal meal, as you're still recovering. Besides, I shared a large dinner with my brother last night."

Lydia watched the activity of Youngston and the footmen. Not formal? When Harrison sat before her, resplendent in his traditional black wear, and crystal goblets and china plates sat on the table? Even the tablecloth matched the floral pattern of the curtains.

Her fingers trailed across the sterling silver flatware. No, she was not used to this, which made her uncomfortable.

Too jarring. Until last week, Lydia slept in alleys.

Since awakening and finding herself in this town house, she felt strange, removed from reality. It could be the fever, for she still had a slight one. Surely all this could not be real, Harrison included.

Was this a fairytale dream born from her secret hopes and imaginings? Or had she died and gone to heaven?

Silly thoughts, but Lydia knew how sickness and high fever could warp reality.

The food here was beyond compare. A footman placed a bowl of chowder with bits of carrot, celery, potato, and shrimp before Lydia. Watching what spoon Harrison used, as there were three utensils at her setting, she did the same and daintily slurped a spoonful.

She supposed she should say something. "You have a brother living nearby?"

"Yes. My middle brother, Tremain, is a few streets away at the Gransford town house."

Harrison explained about his ex-vicar, war veteran, and viscount brother. It was a struggle to keep up with the conversation, especially the confusing details on how he became a viscount.

No, she was not recovered from this illness by any stretch. The audible rattle in her chest and the hoarseness of her voice were proof of that. And the coughing fits. Pray she did not take one during dinner.

"And you serve in the House of Lords as well? I thought those with a courtesy title were not permitted to attend." Or are they? It was all so muddled.

"Those with a courtesy title do not, but the queen ennobled me. That honor will not pass on to any of my heirs. It allows me to attend and serve in the House of Lords. It is indeed rare for a duke and his two sons to be serving at the same time. There is no denying that the queen favors our family, much to the chagrin of others. We take our responsibilities seriously and work diligently to make Great Britain the envy of the world. Though there is much work to be done concerning the poor."

Lydia murmured in agreement, for she had lived it firsthand. Anyone could wind up on the streets due to fate and circumstance—a scary prospect.

The servants whisked away the empty bowls, and a plate of meat and vegetables replaced them. They had skipped several courses, and Lydia was glad. Her appetite still was not what it should be.

"A hearty roast beef. Please, do not stand on ceremony. Tuck in." Harrison gave her a teasing smile.

Cutting her meat, she asked, "Is the viscount your only sibling?"

"No, I have a younger brother, Spencer." He paused; his look turned reflective. "Spence is special. He had many issues growing up, so much so that the physicians wanted him in the asylum. Children's psychosis, the experts called it. My father would not hear of it." Harrison laid his utensils aside. He explained the manifestations of his brother's condition.

Lydia nodded. "Once at St. Thomas's, a young boy was brought in suffering from much of what you have described. He seemed completely lost in his own world and wouldn't look you in the eye. He hardly seemed aware of what was happening around him or what was said. Then he would react, usually violently."

"And what happened to the lad?" Harrison asked softly.

"The doctor said he must be committed to the asylum at once. The child knew for he began to cry and rage when he heard that word. He spoke for the first time, begging his parents that he not be taken away. It was horrible."

"Spence was not that severe, thank God. But I have noticed he sometimes doesn't look you in the eye. My brother has suffered from outbursts—more frequently as a child—not so much now. If he structures his day and sticks to it, he can keep control of his impulses. He managed to get through school, though Tremain and I were there to assist in any way we could. He is a professor of ancient history. Researching, not teaching."

"How wonderful for him. Is that why you became interested in medical studies, your brother's—I'm not sure what to call it. A condition? A disorder?"

Harrison picked up his utensils and continued eating. "A condition. Yes, it is the reason. My fellow students mocked me mercilessly at Cambridge. Why would an heir to a duke study medicine since it supposedly is beneath me? A middle-class profession. Obviously, I didn't listen."

"Yet, you kept it secret. Is it because of the censure from your peers?"

"Yes and no." He glanced at his butler. "Leave us, Youngston. Return in about thirty minutes."

"Yes, my lord." The butler snapped his fingers at the two footmen, and they were left alone.

"I am sorry. Is your staff not aware of what you do? Did I reveal too much?"

"They are unaware, but I surmise they have a clue. I wish to continue with our secret exchange and—"

A coughing fit interrupted Harrison. She lifted the napkin to her mouth to catch the sputum. How mortifying.

His eyebrows creased with worry. "You're still unwell. You should return to your room to rest as soon as we complete our meal. Are you up for further conversation?"

If Lydia were of a mercenary bent, she could exaggerate her illness. Take advantage of his generous nature by extending her stay and indulging in her beautiful room, servants, food, clothes, and anything else she could squeeze out of him.

But regardless of her sins and mistakes, she was not that shameless and cruel. Glancing at Harrison's handsome face, the concern showing on it touched her.

Lydia could not hurt this caring man, no matter her circumstances.

Wiping her mouth, she nodded. "Yes, please. Let us continue."

"Last night, we left off at what you're accused of. I want to let you know that I've hired an investigator to look into these charges. Mr.

Robins is an ex-copper, a decorated and respected detective sergeant with the Metropolitan Police."

Lydia dropped her fork, and pieces of carrot bounced across the tablecloth. Her heart sank. Then fright settled in the dark corners of her soul. Suppose John Huntsford caught wind of someone asking questions. It did not bear thinking about.

Harrison laid his hand on top of hers. Much-needed comfort and warmth traveled through her.

"Mr. Robins is discreet, do not worry. He knows of the detective who came to the Terminus. He said Willis is an oily character. Willis may be investigating this off the books. The surgeon no doubt hired him. There may not even be official charges against you. Robins will get to the bottom of it."

No charges? Is it possible?

Her stomach lurched, and she brought her hand to her mouth, her eyes closing briefly.

"Lydia? Look at me."

She cracked open her eyes and met his gaze.

"I give you my word that I will assist you in any way I can."

"Why?" she whispered. "You don't know me. I am a stranger. I could be lying—"

"It's easy enough to verify. Robins is doing so as we speak." Harrison removed his hand and continued eating, so she did the same. "Besides—we made a pact. Reveal secrets and tell the truth. And you have so far?"

"Yes."

"So have I."

"You truly are a hero."

Harrison laughed, and the masculine sound reverberated through her, her toes curling with pleasure in her slippers.

"I am not a masked crusader leaping about the rooftops of London, sword in hand, fighting injustice and brutality."

"But you *are* masked. As I said before, you're a medical Robin Hood. Instead of a bow and arrow, you battle injustice with a stethoscope and your vast medical knowledge. You save those who cannot rescue themselves. You rescued me. I will be eternally grateful."

A smile tugged at the corner of his mouth. "Thank you. It was my pleasure."

Lydia picked up her fork. "About the theft of pharmaceuticals. As I said, I had nothing to do with it. When John Huntsford spoke about his twisted plan, I didn't take him seriously. I wish I had. When I found out about the robbery, I confronted him. He warned me to keep quiet, or he would blame it on me and reveal our clandestine relationship."

She blinked, then looked down at her hands. They were trembling. John had then struck her for the first time. The blow was so forceful that it knocked her off her feet. That became the deciding factor in her sudden flight from him.

"And he stated that he would also reveal the salacious details of our arrangement, claiming I was the one who introduced him to drugs through the enticement of sex. I stupidly believed he loved me when all along he used me. And he'd been taking my money. John can be very convincing. I was ashamed. Frightened."

Lydia paused as old horrors clawed their way back to the surface of her mind. She took a breath, buried them again, and continued.

"After...an unpleasant incident between us, I made my escape when he left for work. I had no idea if he'd reported the crime and accused me. I did not stay about to find out. Until the policeman showed up at the Terminus."

"Let us wait to see what Mr. Robins reports. As he said, Huntsford may have hired this Willis to investigate."

Lydia shakily dabbed at her mouth with the napkin. "Huntsford said I was his property, to do with what he will. He had too much control over my life. What I thought was love—it is obvious I know nothing of it. I cannot abide being a victim. But I am, aren't I? I laid my trust in a man who did not deserve it. I gave myself—" she choked back a sob.

"Lydia—"

"I'm utterly and completely ruined, professionally and personally, and I've no one to blame but myself."

"You are not the first to mistakenly place your love and trust in the wrong person," Harrison offered gently.

Lydia met his empathetic gaze. "Have you?"

"I've never been in love. Not even close. I probably never will. Perhaps it is best. I'm embarking on selecting a suitable bride. It's past time I married."

That bit of information caused her to feel more nauseous than she was already. Why did it matter to her if the marquess married? Why wouldn't an heir to a duke want to find someone suitable?

Of which she was not—in any way.

After her disaster with Huntsford, why was she even experiencing any feelings toward the marquess?

Oh, she was shameless.

And so desperate to fill the empty void in her heart, she latched on to any man who showed her any attention.

A fatal flaw, to be sure.

"The opium? Would you elaborate on the usage?" Harrison asked.

No more.

Lydia could not talk about this, not tonight. Her whole body shuddered; goosebumps raised on her flesh. At least she'd eaten most of the food, though it churned in her stomach. How could she discuss opium usage and how it factored into her and Huntsford's physical relations? If he didn't think her a degenerate now, he would once she revealed the facts of her situation. She should never have agreed to the exchange of secrets.

Placing her palms flat on the table, she stood, then swayed. Harrison jumped to his feet and held her steady. Before she could protest, he swept her up in his arms.

"No, Harrison—"

"Hush, I'm taking you upstairs. You're far from recovered, and I should not have asked you to join me tonight. As a physician, I should have known better. Youngston!" he bellowed.

The butler must have been just outside the door, for he opened it.

"Miss Best has taken ill. I'm taking her to her room. Please prepare a brandy toddy, and see that the fire in the hearth is going at full tilt. Have Mariah bring the drink and tell her she will assist Miss Best."

"At once, my lord."

Sighing shakily, she slipped her arms about his neck as he vaulted up the stairs as if she weighed nothing. Lydia was far too thin and weaker than she imagined. The illusion that she was recovering was wishful thinking, and the fact that she nearly swooned at the dinner table was proof.

Harrison lowered her to the bed and then touched her forehead. It felt blessedly cool.

"You're warm. Yes, dressing and coming downstairs were premature. Ah, here is Mrs. Wickes."

"I've come to assist. Mariah will be bringing the toddy directly. What can I do?" the housekeeper asked.

"See that Miss Best is comfortable. Anything she needs." He removed his hand and straightened. "Have the maid fetch her food and books or leave her to sleep." Harrison trailed a finger across her flushed cheek. "I will check in later this evening when I return."

"Har...my lord, you are going to—" Lydia let the sentence hang in the air, for she would keep his secrets. No doubt he was going to the Terminus.

"Yes. I am. Rest and recover."

He stepped away from the bed, turned, and left the room.

Never had a man cared for her like this, not since her father. Sniffling quietly as Mrs. Wickes tended the fire, she allowed another moment of self-pity.

She would never find a man like Harrison. For any decent man of honor, society considered her ruined. Focus on getting well; the sooner she recovered, the sooner she would be far from here and the temptation of the Marquess of Tennington.

Whatever lay in her future, she was determined to move forward with her head held high, battered but all the wiser from the lessons she gleaned from her various life-altering mistakes.

Returning to medicine may be an uphill battle, but it was one she was willing to make.

Reparations. Recovery. To start anew.

She would take it if the marquess offered his assistance and be eternally grateful.

Closing off her heart, however, was an absolute must.

Chapter 15

ARRIVING AT THE TERMINUS shortly after nine o'clock, Harrison immediately threw himself into work. Safely hidden behind his Doctor Damian façade, he treated dozens of people, assessed the new arrivals, and received a status update from Sister Monica.

At midnight, Sam strolled in. His friend didn't bother to conceal his identity. Harrison envied his freedom.

Sam motioned toward the small office area, and Harrison nodded. Once out of sight, Harrison pulled off the mask.

"Why are you here so late?" he asked Sam.

"I was on my way home from a secret meeting with a certain young lady."

Harrison raised an eyebrow. "You have a new mistress?"

Sam snickered. "I never had an old one. I'm not flush enough to support such an expensive venture. This encounter was entirely innocent." Sam took a seat opposite Harrison. "I met her at that blasted ball we recently attended."

"The dark-haired beauty I saw you talking to? And she agreed to meet you? How bold. Who is she?" Harrison asked.

"Adelia Wollstonecraft, youngest daughter of Viscount Tensbridge."

"Jesus, Sam. You are aware her grandfather, the Earl of Carnstone, attended the meeting with Shaftsbury regarding our clinic."

Sam crossed his arms. "And?"

Yes, and what?

The Wollstonecrafts were not an arrogant clan. The family was just as passionate about progressive causes as the Hornsbys.

"Meeting any young lady in secret is not very prudent. Scandal and all that societal rot."

"I am aware," Sam replied. "We wanted to become better acquainted before we ventured further. I haven't even kissed her as yet. I will do what is proper soon enough, like calling on her at home and meeting her parents, older brothers, and sister. What do you know about the viscount? Will he object to a country-raised physician with no name or money to court his daughter?"

Harrison tore off his gloves and tossed them on the makeshift desk. "We've had dealings with the Wollstonecrafts but haven't interacted much in society, at least not of late. We collaborated on a home for those with special needs near our estate. They rarely came to London except to Westminster and only then when necessary. Who was she with at the ball? I assume that someone chaperoned her."

"By her great aunt and uncle, Garrett and Abigail Wollstonecraft. They were nearby when we spoke. Her uncle is a beast of a man. Half Scottish, Adelia said. He must be six and a half feet tall and solid as a brick wall. I wouldn't want to cross him. Anyway, Adelia is heading to Kent tomorrow to the family estate. Hence the reason we wanted to meet. We've agreed to correspond."

Sam sighed wistfully. "My God, no woman has affected me like this before. The ease with which we converse. The way she makes my heart pound. Never have I felt so alive."

Yes. Alive.

Exactly how he felt when he was with Lydia.

"Then, by all means, Sam, follow your heart. I doubt the Wollstonecrafts would hold it against you regarding your lack of money. They are rich enough and will no doubt settle a dowry on their daughter. Miss Adelia is aware you're but a poor doctor?"

Sam chuckled. "I told her; she never batted an eye. Already I like and admire her beyond her outward beauty. Enough about me. Will you be following your own advice? And don't give me that blather about duty."

"Perhaps I should inquire if the Wollstonecrafts have any other eligible and unmarried young ladies in the family," Harrison replied wryly.

"Or perhaps you should follow your heart. I take it Miss Best has not absconded with the silver? No? Good. Learn all you can about her. Do not deny the feelings within; I cannot picture you in one of those damned aristo-alliance marriages. What a cold and lonely outlook. You deserve more."

"So I've been told. I will heed your advice as best as I'm able." Harrison stood and affixed the mask and reached for his coat. "I believe I will head home. You can finish up here?"

"Absolutely. I'm on call at St. Bart's for the next three days in the casualty ward from two in the afternoon until midnight. I'll come here first in the morning. It will leave the afternoons without either of us if you attend Parliament. I've already informed the nuns, and they said they will fill in where possible."

Sam exhaled. "You are right; it is becoming impossible for us to keep up this crushing and punishing pace. Let us pursue this clinic with all haste. For all our sakes, the nuns included."

Harrison nodded as he slipped on his coat. He kept the mask on until he was outside. Then he would walk a pace from the Terminus before he removed it and hailed a hansom cab.

"I agree. Goodnight, Sam, do not stay too late."

"I won't. I'll send word when I hear from William Robins. Should be any day now."

Harrison escaped, and once he stepped on the footpath, he removed the cap and mask. It was dark, and no one was about.

Sam and Adelia Wollstonecraft.

He knew nothing of the young lady. But he knew the family well enough that he would be honored to put in a good word on his friend's behalf, should he require it.

Life was moving forward for them both.

The clop-clop of horses' hooves filled his hearing, and he hailed it when the hansom came into view. On the way home, his discussion with Sam filled his thoughts.

He honestly had no idea what to do next, personal or professional.

Once he entered the town house, Youngston dutifully met him at the door.

"I have told you before there is no need to wait up for me," Harrison stated.

"I understand, my lord. Do you require any assistance? Gillis has retired for the night. I insisted."

Harrison handed his coat to Youngston. He never reacted to Harrison coming in at all hours dressed in white. He often wondered if his staff discussed his schedule, absences, and stranger dress.

After Lydia's slight slip, Youngston had undoubtedly put the pieces together. And the fact that the housekeeper told Lydia that a doctor had attended to her.

Meaning him.

What did it matter? The servants were discreet, and he trusted them all unreservedly.

"No, lock up for the night. I can see to my own needs."

"Very well, my lord."

Harrison quietly ascended the stairs, stopping outside Lydia's room. He turned the knob and peered in. The room lay in darkness, and the fire banked.

About to close the door, a voice reached him.

"My lord?"

"Yes, just checking to see if you are all right. Go back to sleep."

"Come in for a moment. Leave the light low, please. What I have to say, I would rather have the protective darkness."

Stepping across the threshold, he closed the door behind him. It was blasted dark, but he headed in the general direction of the bed. Groping about, Harrison located the chair and sat next to her.

"What we spoke of," Lydia said, her voice shaky. "The usage. I have to tell someone to get this off my conscience. I'm unsure where to begin except to blurt it out. John started to rub cocaine on our privates. 'To enhance the experience,' he said. Huntsford then wanted to introduce me to inject it directly into the vein. I balked. He forced me to take the drug mixture—I despised it. I began to abhor him. It's as you said; it was a violation. Though he never forced himself on me physically, he assaulted me nonetheless."

Anger boiled inside Harrison at the thought of this lovely woman suffering abuse. The temptation to hunt down this reprobate doctor and throttle him senseless was hard to ignore.

"An assault, to be certain, and I am deeply sorry a man treated you thus."

"Yet I stayed. Not long after this horrible incident, but still. What does that say about me?"

"You believe in your craft as a nurse. You wanted to fix or cure him, creating an unhealthy bond between you."

A gasping sob escaped Lydia. "Yes. Exactly. But it's beyond that. I should have left when he first introduced drugs into our relationship. I became addicted to the numbing sensations and the wild and heightened sensual responses. I am a deviant. There is no hope for me." Her voice was low, and Harrison could hear the shame in her tone.

"I've heard of what you've described. Cocaine is absorbed through the skin. Numbing prolongs the act. It wasn't necessarily the sex you craved but the drug itself. When did you last take the cocaine mixture?"

"The injection? Close to two weeks before I gathered enough courage to depart. After forcing the needle into my arm, I refused to allow Huntsford to touch me. I was silently relieved that he had left me alone. He was no doubt finding his thrills elsewhere. There were nights he did not come home, and I was glad. I should have left then, but I had nowhere to go. There was hardly any money left. I'd been frightened into inaction. That is not like me at all. My father—"

Another sob escaped her. "Papa would be so disappointed in me. It was not the way he raised me. He was a kind and honorable man."

Harrison reached into the dark and found her hand, lacing his fingers through hers.

"Enough punishing yourself. You're away from Huntsford. You need never see or interact with him again. First, we will see what Mr. Robins has discovered and plan from there. There is no reason you cannot find employment as a nurse somewhere and move on with your life."

"Do you think it's possible? Truly? I'm not certain that I can forgive myself."

"One day at a time. It would be best if you recovered from pneumonia, dehydration, and malnutrition first. Worry has brought much of this on and being on the streets these past weeks."

"I do not deserve your kind generosity, but I'm not proud. I will take any assistance you offer, and thank you." She squeezed his hand. "The exchange of secrets appears to be all on my side of the scale. I apologize for this unburdening."

"Do you feel better?"

"As a matter of fact, I do. I doubt there is anything similar in your past."

"Not necessarily. Years ago, in my early twenties, my brother Tremain and I shared a courtesan. Opium and spirits fueled the experience, and it left me empty. I never touched the drug again. The gossip cemented my reputation, and I used it as a shield for pursuing my doctoring. My life is built on a lie." Harrison released her hand. "But that is a conversation for another night."

"When I am well enough, and if the police do not hunt me, may I come and assist you at the Terminus? Volunteering would ease my guilt, but I will repay you for all you've done for me."

"I do not expect payment of any kind."

There was an edge to his voice; he couldn't help it. Just what did Lydia think he would demand in recompense?

Lydia remained silent for several minutes. Should he take his leave?

"I meant no offense. I want to do something useful. From what I observed, you could use the assistance."

She wasn't wrong.

"Yes, we could. Very well. Once we have the lay of the land and we feel your recovery is at hand, we will broach the subject again. Agreed?"

"Yes. Thank you."

Harrison stood. About to depart, he hesitated. He could vaguely make out her shape in the shadows, so he leaned in and laid his hand against her forehead. Warm, but at least it was not raging hot.

Without thinking, he kissed her temple, and a soft sigh escaped her lips. The sound spurred him forward. He gently kissed her cheek, then laid his lips against hers, barely touching, but enough to cause a roll of heat to travel through him.

"Sleep well," he murmured as he straightened.

"Thank you for listening. And not judging."

Harrison left the room, closing the door softly.

Later, as he lay in bed, the heated sensation of the brief kiss stayed with him, jolting his heart—the conversation they had shared played over and over in his mind.

Good God, what she had revealed.

An unhealthy bond was the right of it. Harrison was not a prude. He wasn't shocked by the fact that she had sex with Huntsford. After all, Lydia had believed she was in love and that they would have a future.

Considering the circumstances, it was a good thing she never married him. It would be a damned sight harder to extricate herself from the man if she had.

Regardless, no matter what lay in her past, he was developing deep feelings for Lydia and wasn't sure what to think about it.

Fatigue got the best of him, and he gave himself over to sleep. His dreams were filled once again with a complicated golden-haired beauty.

LYDIA AWOKE TO FEEL rested and more at peace in ages. Confession is good for the soul, or so she'd heard.

Rising from the bed, she yawned and went to the window. Pulling aside the curtains, she peered out. The street below was alive with vendors pushing carts laden with loaves of bread, fresh fruit, or flowers. Ladies in fancy dresses carrying matching parasols strolled along the sidewalks either with other young ladies or with a gentleman.

It was a beautiful spring day, and the idyllic life unfolding before was almost too good to be true. Even the birds were singing.

Eleven days had passed since her rescue from the alley, but the memory of being alone on the streets still haunted her. It may haunt her for the rest of her days.

Every time she awakened, it took her several moments to realize she was not sleeping on the streets but in a comfortable bed with expensive linens and a feather pillow. A knock sounded at the door.

"Yes?"

"May I come in?"

It was Harrison.

Good lord, facing him in the harsh daylight after her late-night confession would be embarrassing, to say the least. But Lydia was determined to put her past firmly behind her. Reaching for her wrap, she slipped it on as she headed toward the door.

Upon opening it, her breath seized momentarily at the sight of him. Immaculately groomed and dressed as always, the warm smile making the lines crinkle at the corner of his eyes appealed the most.

How tempting it would be to curl up in his embrace. Nuzzle against his perfectly tied cravat. Inhale the masculine scent of his lime and bergamot cologne.

"You look rested. I wondered if you were well enough to join me for breakfast. The staff laid a veritable feast on the sideboard, and I need assistance eating said banquet." He gave her a teasing wink.

"I would like to give it a go."

"I'll send Mariah up immediately. You slept well?"

"Yes. Thank you."

"Your cough has all but vanished. A good sign."

Their gazes locked. The heat emanating from them could light the logs in the hearth. Goodness, Harrison radiated virile masculinity. And he caused Lydia's body to react from the tingling of her nerve endings to the flutter in her stomach—and lower.

Two of his fingers wrapped around a strand of her golden tresses. "I like your hair down. Beautiful."

She sucked in a breath at the feel of him caressing her hair. Harrison stood close enough that she could nuzzle his neck. Lord, she was mightily tempted.

"I will see you directly."

He lowered his hand and departed, and then Lydia exhaled.

By the time she dressed and a footman escorted her to the dining room, she managed to rein in her runaway emotions.

Harrison stood as soon as she entered. The sideboard held many several silver chafing dishes. A footman stood at the ready to assist.

"Come and make your selection," Harrison smiled. "There are not huge amounts, as I believe in conserving and not wasting food, but there is enough for you to find something you like."

Harrison handed her a plate as she lifted one of the dishes. Selecting poached eggs, bacon, fruit, and a scone, she took her seat as the footman automatically filled her cup with tea.

"That's all, William. Inform Youngston we are not to be disturbed for about thirty minutes."

"Yes, my lord."

Lydia cut into the egg and popped a piece in her mouth. Lovely, made with shredded cheese.

"I received word this morning that Mr. Robins wishes to meet tomorrow. I could ask him to come here so you may sit in on the discussion."

And have her personal life picked over by a stranger while in her presence?

How mortifying.

It struck her as she ate after all that happened, her love and confidence destroyed by Huntsford—she trusted Harrison Hornsby.

Was she making another grave mistake? So grateful for the rescue that she would believe anything he told her? Was she taken in by his generous nature and the molten heat radiating in his silver-gray eyes?

His gentle kiss? His heroic doings as Doctor Damian?

Blast, she hated doubting herself. But she could no longer cower. How could she move forward if she didn't confront the past?

"Yes, have Mr. Robins come here. I will attend the meeting."

Harrison gave her an admiring look. "Brave girl. Well done."

She laughed brokenly. "Brave? Hardly. I merely want to put this behind me."

"If all works out the way I believe it will, there is no reason you can't move on with your life immediately."

Harrison sipped his tea. "There is to be a double wedding in about two weeks. My brothers will be marrying their brides-to-be. What I'm about to reveal about my family is part of the exchange of secrets.

Despite the gossip, I protect my family as best as I can. I would protect them with my life."

"You have my word. I will not repeat anything you tell me."

As they ate, he elucidated how his younger brother Spencer met his choice of bride. An ex-madam? How fascinating.

Then he explained about Tremain and the ex-governess. Harrison hinted at her dismissal from her post because of a dalliance with the son of the house. But he spoke of both women in glowing terms stating that the couples deserved all the happiness in the world.

"What captivating stories. Your brothers found love matches in the most unlikely of circumstances."

"Yes, I couldn't be more pleased for them."

"Are your brothers marrying here in London?" she asked.

"No. I'm leaving for Hastings just before the nuptials. The affair will be at my family's country estate near the town. Never fear. Whatever news Robins imparts, I will ensure all is well before I head off."

Is he leaving? Her heart sank.

Harrison had no interest in her despite the heated looks they'd exchanged. Perhaps the gentle kiss last night was innocent, after all.

As usual, she read too much into it.

Lydia did not reply but instead pulled her protective wall about her. She must remain politely distant until he departed for Hastings and had no business daydreaming that there could be more, considering his brothers' choices of brides. For a brief moment, she allowed the fantasy of Harrison and her—oh, it was madness.

The crestfallen look on her face must be evident.

"Are you all right, Lydia?" Harrison asked.

Her counterfeit smile froze in place. "Yes. All is well."

But it wasn't.

Lydia would not show her vulnerable side again.

Or expose her heart.

Chapter 16

HARRISON INSTRUCTED William Robins to come to the town house at eleven in the morning. Harrison had a busy day ahead, attending the session at Parliament and then his shift at the terminus.

Sam's shifts at St. Bart's were causing havoc, and if the hospital took his friend on permanently, it would cause further tribulations.

It was only a matter of time, for Sam was more than competent, and Harrison suspected his dear friend hadn't looked earnestly for a position so he could continue assisting at the terminus.

Though he'd offered more than once to have Sam move into the town house and have Harrison pay him a stipend, his proud friend refused. Instead, he stayed at a small rooming house, supplementing his income with sporadic shifts at various London hospitals.

But now that he'd met Miss Wollstonecraft, Sam would have to consider a different trajectory for his future. Harrison would never stand in the way of his close friend's career.

Yes, immediate changes were needed.

The sooner he discussed this situation with his family, the sooner he could go public.

Once settled in the parlor, Harrison's gaze moved to Lydia. She sat ramrod straight on the settee. Has something happened since yesterday morning?

Harrison could not pinpoint what.

She was polite, but their effortless, conversational intimacy had disappeared. Last night she retired early and took dinner in her room.

Robins sat on the divan opposite and refused the offer of tea. And he refused to give his coat to Youngston. Robins fidgeted, flipping through the pages of his notebook, clearly uncomfortable. Not used to such surroundings, or did he have bad news to impart?

"The theft of drugs at St. Thomas Hospital occurred thirteen days ago, long after Miss Chesterton departed. So far, the hospital is keeping the theft quiet; they believe someone in-house did the deed. They're questioning staff, especially those with access to the keys to the various medicine cabinets. Opium, cocaine, and morphine were part of the inventory taken."

Robins looked up from his notebook and met Lydia's gaze. "There has been no police report—nor have you been named officially as a suspect, Miss Chesterton."

A gasp of relief escaped Lydia. Then she quickly collected her emotions and held them in check.

Robins glanced down at his notes. "However, the staff and administrators are genuinely concerned about your disappearance. I suggest you write a note to those in charge, claiming you had to leave London due to an emergency. Offer your resignation with the hope that you may contact them for a reference in the future. Make your apologies for the sudden departure and whatnot. I think it best you establish a timeframe and reason for your exodus to further separate you from the theft." Robins flipped through the pages of his notebook as if searching for information.

"I concur. Miss Chesterton, what Mr. Robins suggested is prudent. We can find you employment elsewhere, far from Mr. Huntsford," Harrison interjected.

She gave him a wan smile in reply.

"And now we come to Surgeon Huntsford," Robins said. "It's not a pretty tale. He has disappeared from his residence. He sold what possessions remained in the place and departed in the dead of night. Was the rent in arrears, Miss Chesterton?"

Lydia flushed, clearly embarrassed. "Yes, I tried to keep up with current payments."

"I spoke to the landlord; he was quite angry, for Huntsford sold a few pieces of furniture that belonged to the flat. I encouraged him to place a debt collector after Huntsford, for the total debt is more than ten pounds, grounds for incarceration in a debtors' prison. It would be one way to pursue justice. The surgeon's current residence is a squalid room in Whitechapel with a Miss Fannie Slickson, where one of my men found out; he has stayed on several occasions."

Lydia's flush deepened.

So, her lover cheated on her. Harrison was not surprised.

"As for his position at St. Thomas Hospital," Robins continued flatly, "He works four shifts in a row, then takes several off. It's during this period that he indulges in his vices. At work, he's sober and competent enough not to arouse suspicion. There is also no suspicion surrounding him regarding the theft. You believe it was him, Miss Chesterton?"

"Huntsford always managed to put on a public face of respectability. I'm not surprised. But he had discussed the robbery in length. He talked of not stealing the keys but making wax impressions and having keys made. You see, he thought to take a little here and there. I explained that a nurse does the inventory at the end of every shift, and they would notice if even a small amount were missing. He must have decided to take it all in one lot." Lydia frowned, her brows knotting in worry. "Oh, my. Does that make me an accessory to the crime?"

"The hospital and the police could see it that way, Miss Chesterton. And it is why you must send that letter immediately."

"How can it be proven that he's behind the theft?" Lydia asked.

"There is no way to verify this burglary unless a witness saw him," Robins replied. "Unless you testified in court, which means—"

"My sordid past with him would be publicly exposed—my lack of character and courage. I should have approached the head nurse about this when he started planning his reprehensible scheme. But I didn't want to reveal our relationship. At first, I didn't believe him. I only considered my safety and self-preservation when I realized he was serious. How utterly selfish. The first moment I could, I escaped."

"He has privately hired Willis as I originally thought. Why, Miss Chesterton, would Huntsford seek you out at this juncture? Desperate enough to find you that he hired a copper for the job?" Robins asked.

Lydia wrung her hands in what Harrison guessed was agitation. This incident must be highly discomforting to relive, but he admired her honesty.

"He's claimed on more than one occasion that I am his possession. From what I know about him, he's angry I've left, misses the control he wielded, and misses my steady income. He wants me back under his thumb. Huntsford believes it is his right."

She bit her lower lip. "I would be a handy person to blame the theft on should suspicion turn his way. I now understand that Huntsford is the type of man who would metaphorically throw me under the wheels of a moving carriage to protect himself."

Robins turned to Harrison. "What do you wish to do, my lord? I can have this landlord report the debt immediately. Give up his location. He would be arrested and held until his hearing in debtor's court. It would give us time to decide how to proceed. As in bringing further charges." Robins tucked his notebook in his side pocket. "We would need more proof than Miss Chesterton's testimony. No offense, miss."

"Would he have the drugs on him?" Harrison asked. "He could be arrested for possessing the stolen goods."

"Ah, true, my lord. But we inspected the room when the occupants visited the local pub. We could find nothing beyond the paraphernalia that arises from frequent drug use. An opium pipe and needles are not evidencing enough to indicate his involvement in the theft. Huntsford is clever by keeping his stash private. Miss Slickson may not even be aware. She also works when the surgeon works, if you understand my meaning. Huntsford would not want to keep his drugs in such a public place. She has men visiting at all hours during his hospital shifts."

Harrison glanced at Lydia; she was flushing furiously. His doctor's mind turned to the possibility of sexual diseases. As a nurse, she must be well aware of the risks. Had she had unprotected sex with this Huntsford, a man who was indiscriminate with his choice of partners?

"What do you wish to do, Miss Chesterton?" Harrison asked.

She met his gaze. "About Huntsford?"

"Yes."

A furrow appeared between her brows, and he and Robins waited patiently for her reply. It was not for them to decide on her fate. The choice must be hers.

"If it's all the same to you, my lord, I believe it best not to show our hand too soon. All Huntsford would have to do is sell the drugs in his possession, and he would be able to pay his debt and avoid incarceration," Lydia said, her voice firm.

Robins nodded. "Very true, although this may be one way to catch him with the pharmaceutical goods. Him trying to sell them. We should keep that avenue open."

"I agree," Harrison said. "Continue with your surveillance, Robins. Gather as much information as you can."

"I will testify," Lydia interjected. "About his vile habits and his thievery plan."

Robins nodded as he removed the notebook from his pocket and scribbled in it.

Harrison smiled.

That's my brave girl.

His admiration grew, along with more intense emotions becoming harder to ignore.

"Then, if there is nothing else, my lord, I will take my leave." Robins stood.

"Do stay in touch. Youngston?"

The butler stepped into the room. "Yes, my lord?"

"Please escort Mr. Robins to the front entrance. Anytime he or his men come to the door, they will be admitted immediately without question."

"Yes, my lord. Mr. Robins?"

After slipping his notebook into his side pocket, he reached for his cane, then touched his forelock.

"My lord. Miss Chesterton."

Once alone, Lydia buried her face in her hands, her delicate shoulders shaking.

Harrison immediately moved to her side and gathered her into his embrace.

"The police are not pursuing you. You are not a suspect. Not all is lost, Lydia."

She sniffled against his coat and nodded. After several moments, Lydia laid her hands against his chest and gently pushed him away.

Harrison grasped her chin and met her gaze. Her eyes were red, her lower lip trembling.

"What is it? What is going on, Lydia? Why did you take your meal in your room last night? Why are you pulling away from me?"

"I don't know where to begin."

"We've been honest with each other, don't stop now."

She gazed up at him, sadness reflected in her eyes. "I wish I'd met you two years ago, but how and where? You're the heir to a duke. Our paths would never have crossed. I became upset when you mentioned your search for a wife. How completely inappropriate."

Lydia sighed wistfully. "I'm attracted to you, and I have no business saying this to you, let alone feeling it. I thought it best to keep my distance. You see, I must take control of my life once again. I must stop living in fear. I no longer wish to be this scared, cowed woman."

Harrison's heart soared at her declaration of being attracted to him.

"I don't make of habit of seducing vulnerable women. Or bring them to my home. But I have, haven't I? Perhaps not the seducing part, but I've wanted to. God, how I've wanted to. The attraction is mutual. What do we do now?" he murmured.

"I'll take your offer of assistance in finding me a nursing position far from here. And I believe we should do this as soon as possible."

Well.

Harrison released her chin. "You're hardly recovered enough to take such a step forward."

"I'm feeling stronger with each passing day. Perhaps we could find me a position in a town or village; I could take a room nearby and continue to recover. I will reimburse you as soon as I'm earning my way. Meanwhile, I would still like to assist you at the terminus. I need to feel useful and be able to pay you back in some way for your generosity and kindness."

Pain sliced through his heart, and he didn't like the sensation.

"However, entering into an affair with me is not the way you wish to 'pay me back.'"

Her eyes widened. "Affair?"

"Have I insulted you? I do apologize. There is nothing I wish for more than having you in my bed. In my arms. But I would never insist on it or take it as payment. I would want you to come to me of your own accord. Because you want me. Desire me. No other reason."

Her expression remained a combination of shock and trepidation.

Hang it. Harrison should have kept his desires to himself.

She'd just left a toxic and abusive relationship. Lydia needed time to heal not only physically but mentally and emotionally.

God, he was a selfish bastard.

What possessed him to speak so? Reveal his true feelings?

Hell, he was well-versed in hiding his emotions in most situations. Lydia broke apart all the barriers—the ones he'd spent years building.

"Forget I said that—any of it. I cannot believe I even suggested an affair. Chalk it up to the inane utterings of an arrogant, entitled peer. Again, I offer my deepest apologies." Harrison stood. "I must take my leave. I've had numerous appointments this afternoon. I'll return for dinner at seven. Will you join me?"

"Yes."

Lydia answered in a firm voice, no trembling or fluttering that he could see or hear.

Embarrassed, he gave her a stiff bow and exited the room before he made a further fool of himself. As he rushed outside, he laid a hand against his cheek. The skin burned red-hot. Anger for showing his vulnerable side, and damn it all, he did have one. Harrison caught a hansom cab and instructed the driver to take him to The Red Lion pub.

Waiting for him in the corner booth were Sam and William Robins. Harrison slid across the seat, a pint of bitter already sitting on the table for him. He needed the libation after that awkward conversation with Lydia.

During the short journey, he arranged his features into detached indifference. In other words, the bored look of a peer.

"I ordered the pies," Sam said. "William has brought me up to date. Quite the tale."

"Yes, quite."

Harrison was still annoyed by his conversation with Lydia and answered Sam a little too sharply. His friend, who knew him well, wisely let it pass.

"Well? The remainder of your report, Mr. Robins?"

The man's battered notebook sat on the table before him. "Regarding Lydia Chesterton: her reputation at St. Thomas is stellar. I discovered that she was being discussed for promotion to an operating theater nurse. Before they could formally offer the position, she disappeared. As far as I could glean, she was a private person. No one knew of her personal life. I investigated her previous address, and she lived there with her widower schoolmaster father until his death. Everything that she relayed to you is the truth."

Harrison was silently relieved. He wouldn't have proposed an affair with a woman he didn't trust, but it was gratifying to learn his judgment of her character was not misplaced.

"Thank you, Mr. Robins, for your due diligence. Keep your surveillance on Huntsford." Harrison took a long draw on his pint.

"Don't thank me yet, my lord. I regret to inform you that the surveillance may have been compromised. I admonish myself for using a new employee. The young man believes an unknown person followed him but cannot be sure. You may want to remain cautious. I can place a man on you to see that you are not being followed. No extra charge, of course."

Harrison's blood boiled at a dangerous heat. Damn it all. This man was supposed to be one of the best.

Sliding his gaze to Sam, his annoyance grew. He'd hired this man at his friend's recommendation. Sam gave him a sheepish, apologetic look.

"You're annoyed, my lord, and I don't blame you. I assure you that my work is usually not this slipshod." Mr. Robins looked contrite.

"Followed where, exactly?"

"Again, my man is not certain."

Harrison pushed the pint away from him. He didn't like the sounds of this. Not at all. He glanced about the boisterous pub. There were clusters of men sitting at tables and standing at the bar. Any one of them could be Huntsford or someone he hired.

"You've seen Huntsford, have you not?" he asked Robins.

"From a distance. The man is not here. I checked. Nor was I followed. I'm quite skilled at throwing off the scent. The man is six feet in height, lean, brown hair, longish, here to the collar." Robins pointed to the collar of his coat. "A rumpled appearance, often unshaven. Sometimes wears spectacles, sometimes not. He is good-looking enough to attract women but has a hard way about him. A cruel slant to his mouth. Altogether unsavory."

Harrison knew the type. Malicious to the core, cold-hearted. Caring only for their comforts.

How Lydia could give her heart to such a man—usually, these men were charm incarnate until they got what they wanted.

A barmaid delivered the pies to the table, and Harrison turned his attention to his meal. Could this Huntsford be dangerous? Or, like most of these men, making threats without following them through?

Best to remain cautious.

Across the pub, a man with a beard sat nursing a pint while closely watching them. Harrison glared at him in return. Hard to ascertain his hair color as he wore a cap, though the beard was black. The man looked away. Was he being paranoid? Yes, vigilance would be prudent.

Harrison cut into his pie. "Have a man watch my residence and follow my movements."

"Yes, my lord. I will undertake some of the surveillance personally."

A roll of unease blazed through Harrison. Along with the undeniable urge to protect Lydia at all costs.

And by God, he would.

FOUR DAYS LATER, FEELING much recovered, Lydia sat in Harrison's study at his large oak desk, pen and paper before her. The staff was consistently polite but cast a wary eye her way on occasion as if protecting their employer. She couldn't fault them.

Youngston had brought her afternoon tea on a tray, so she nibbled on a biscuit while collecting her thoughts.

How to describe the relief she felt that the police didn't seek her? A weight had lifted from her tortured soul. But it only gave a modicum of comfort, for there was still much they had to work out.

As for this note, she would do as Mr. Robins suggested, write the hospital, apologizing for her sudden disappearance, and ensure they would provide a reference when needed—once settled in another district. Dipping the pen into the ink, she scratched out sincere reparations.

What excuse? Illness?

It wasn't exactly a lie, for she was sick to her soul. She'd caught a fever that had prevented her from making common sense judgments. But that fever passed, and her mind was clear for the first time in many months. She wrote a brief, but heartfelt note, using illness as an impetus, and stated that she was recovering.

Not actually a lie considering the bout of mild pneumonia.

Lydia also wrote that she was so ill that she could not contact the hospital. She resigned, for she would seek employment elsewhere once recovered. Lydia sincerely thanked the hospital for their faith in her; then signed her name.

Folding the paper in half, she slipped it into the envelope. How to mail it? Lord, she couldn't even afford the postage, for she had no penny to her name.

Harrison would know what to do.

An affair.

Harrison had caught her completely off guard. It is all she had thought about the past few days.

Yes, she assumed he was attracted to her, and Lydia reciprocated the feeling—but an affair? She was not insulted by the suggestion. There was no denying the temptation.

No. Not at this time—if at all.

And judging by Harrison's reaction, it was apparent he regretted the suggestion as soon as he made it. His apology was sincere, and his embarrassment was palatable.

Too much had happened.

Lydia could not expose her defenseless heart to another man, no matter how he appealed. And Harrison did, in so many ways.

"Excuse me, Miss Best?"

Lydia turned in her chair. Youngston stood in the doorway.

"Yes?"

"His lordship has sent word he will not be able to make it for dinner. He said you may have yours in the dining room or a tray in your room, whatever you choose."

Harrison was no doubt admonishing himself for suggesting an affair and would continue to keep his distance. He attended dinner that first night, though there wasn't much conversation, but since?

He obviously regretted his proposal.

How could she come to such a conclusion about him in only a couple of weeks' acquaintance? The flush of his cheeks was ample proof. And the fact she hadn't seen him since.

Perhaps she was not the only one with vulnerabilities. She should take Harrison's withdrawal as a blessing, for the last thing Lydia wished to do was to frustrate or anger him by declining his proposition.

"I will take a tray in my room. Thank you."

The sooner they arranged for her to take employment elsewhere, the better.

Protect my heart.

Lydia had no other choice.

Chapter 17

HARRISON MUST RETURN home sooner rather than later. For all his proclamations that he was not a coward, he was the epitome of one at the moment.

He acted like a hurt, spoiled child.

During the past four days, he kept his distance from Lydia. He'd stayed all night at the Terminus and done so the night before last.

Swaying on his feet, it was past noon, and he was ready to collapse.

"Right you are." Sister Monica clasped his elbow and pulled him toward the office.

She was blasted strong for a woman, or perhaps he was in such a weakened condition that the older nun could take charge and practically drag him across the floor. Regardless, he didn't fight her.

"That is more than enough, your lordship," she whispered fiercely in his ear. "You're dead on your feet."

She steered him into the chair, then closed the makeshift door.

"Harrison, you have me worried. What's going on, my dear? You have the look of a man tortured by demons."

Tortured by demons—of his making. Yes, it was clear that he was his own worst enemy in several areas of his life.

"I'm avoiding a woman."

Sister Monica's eyebrow arched. "Care to discuss it?"

"With a nun? No, I think not."

"Oh, come now," she scoffed. "You think I was born in this habit? I had a life before taking my vows. A man even courted me."

"My apologies," Harrison murmured wearily. "I made an utterly asinine suggestion to a young woman who deserves better from me."

"Then you must make amends and apologize at once."

"Sound advice."

Sister Monica crossed her arms and frowned. "You haven't taken my last bit of sage advice to heart. Here you are, working yourself into a sickbed—or worse."

Her expression softened. "You cannot treat the world entire. Cure all of its ills. All you can do is make your mark in your small corner of the world. And you have, Harrison. You cannot do more, not without doing serious harm to yourself. Rest here; lay your head on the desk. I'll wake you in two hours, and you must return home. Understand?"

"Yes."

He did as Monica suggested, and the last thing he remembered, she gently laid a blanket across his shoulders.

When the kindly nun roused him close to three hours later, he could depart under his own steam, though his legs still trembled from exhaustion.

Once he arrived home and stepped out of the cab, Youngston and Gillis assisted him upstairs, undressed him, and bundled him into bed.

His dreams were fractured, strange, and borne from bone-numbing fatigue. In his nightmare, he attended a fancy ball in his Doctor Damian outfit; his apron spattered with blood. He tried to gain the attention of the lords and ladies, but they looked away in disgust.

Wake up, you fool.

Apparently, he cared what society thought of him. What a distasteful discovery. Among the disdainful crowd? His own family. They turned their backs on him. Was he fearful that his family would reject his secret life? It made no sense. His family always championed good causes.

No, it wasn't only his secretive doctor duties but all the lies he'd told. Harrison should have been forthright about it. What a hash he'd made of things.

Damn all the obstacles. Damn all rationalizations. And damn my craven ways.

Harrison cracked open his eyes and found himself in complete darkness. Someone was in the room with him. He inhaled, and the scent of wildflowers filled his senses.

Lydia lit the gas lamp next to his bed, and golden light surrounded him, causing him to squint.

"It's ten o'clock. At night, obviously," she murmured. "You didn't come home last night. I won't ask where. It's not my business."

"I was at the terminus."

"Oh."

"You thought I was with a woman?" he asked as he rubbed his eyes again, trying to clear the fog from his vision.

Lydia sighed. "I assumed that's where most men go when they storm out. At least, that has been my experience. Especially since you did not come home the night before that."

Harrison sat upright, the blanket slipping to his waist, exposing his bare chest.

Lydia didn't hide her heated look as she inspected him closely. He reveled in the attention. Though he'd lost weight, he still managed to keep himself in reasonable shape.

"Allow me to apologize once again for suggesting an affair. It was borne out of selfishness; I had no business making such a proposal. I offended you. I was embarrassed by my behavior. Overwhelmed with emotion. And, as is typical of me, I kept my distance."

There. I gave a sincerely meant apology once again.

Lydia's gaze traveled upward until it locked with his. "We are a pair, aren't we? When feelings become too much to handle, we withdraw. I wasn't offended. In fact, I was—am—tempted."

His heart thudded double-time at her forthright statement.

"Temptation aside," Lydia continued, "I am not ready for those types of relations. However brief, however passionate. Huntsford has not completely ruined me; I refuse to allow him to achieve such a triumph. I could declare that I will never become involved with another man again. But I won't. No, he will not have that victory over me." Her voice was unwavering, determined.

In truth, Harrison could not fault her reasoning, but his heart throbbed with regret nonetheless. "So not is all lost between us? Or is it wishful thinking on my part?"

"I honestly don't know what the future will bring. I can only stay focused here in the present. I'm not saying no. I am saying—not at this exact time."

Her gaze slid downward; the sheet did not conceal his arousal. "I want to crawl into bed with you, curl up next to your warmth. I want you to hold me and tell me all will be well."

Harrison tossed aside the sheet. "Then come and let me hold you. Regardless of my aroused state, I will not take advantage. You have my word. Do you trust me?"

He was naked. He was exposed—in more ways than one.

Boldly, her gaze slid to that aching and hard part of him. Her admiring look filled him with masculine pride.

"I do trust you, Harrison. If I show moments of doubt or seemingly withdraw, know it's not because of you."

Lydia stood, kicked off her slippers, then lay beside him, facing away from him, on her side. Harrison curled about her, pulling her close. His erection no doubt prodded her back. Lying in his embrace, she didn't flinch or pull away.

The trust was there, taking root, and his heart soared.

Nuzzling her neck, he whispered, "I want you. I want to taste you, every part of your soft skin. I want to be inside you with my cock surrounded and embraced by your warmth. I want to move in out of you, make love to you for hours on end."

Harrison couldn't stay quiet. With Lydia wrapped in his arms like this, the confession spilled out of him. Will she recoil and pull away? Harrison wouldn't blame her if she did.

A soft moan escaped her as she writhed against his stiff shaft. God, he was in blissful agony.

"But it will be on your terms—if you decide you even want me at all," Harrison whispered. "All will be well. I will see to it."

Exhaling shakily, Lydia rubbed her cheek against his arm. There was no reply to his passionate declaration, but her being in his bed like this was enough. They lay together for a long time; he drifted off to sleep again.

Harrison awakened when she pulled from his arms and sat upright.

"Heavens, I fell asleep as well. It's past one in the morning. I'll be heading to my bed. Thank you, Harrison, for understanding. Will we share breakfast?"

"If you wish. Eight o'clock?"

"Yes. May I accompany you to the Terminus in the afternoon? To assist? Please. I am stronger. My voice has all but returned, and the cough has diminished greatly. I need to be useful."

Harrison laid his hand gently against her back. "It is damp below ground. The air is humid and not altogether fresh. It could exacerbate your lung condition. However, you're a nurse, and if you believe you've recovered enough, then accompany me for a few hours by all means."

Turning, Lydia kissed his forehead, picked up her slippers, then hurried from his room, softly closing the door. An innocent kiss and his insides were aflame.

There was no doubt that he'd give her the time she needed. In the interim, he was in absolute anguish.

For he was falling for her, no use denying it. Harrison will have to keep his emotions in check and not overwhelm her.

As for protecting his heart—too blasted late.

FOR THREE DAYS, LYDIA accompanied Harrison to the Terminus. They spent part of the late afternoon and early evening, and she hadn't done much more than serve bowls of soup and assist the nuns with various duties.

On the third day, Harrison tasked her with sorting the newcomers according to medical priority. How pleased she was for Harrison to give her this significant duty.

Sister Monica watched her interaction with Harrison. Obviously, the nun suspected something, for their arrivals and departures were similar. But she was polite and still knew her as Miss Best.

Sitting along the far wall near the entrance were the recent arrivals. Lydia spent time with each one, their stories more heartbreaking than the last. Thankfully, none seemed to be suffering from any severe maladies except dehydration and malnutrition—medical conditions of people experiencing poverty. And excessive weariness.

She stopped before a man wearing patched and torn trousers. He sat on the ground, legs bent, his arms resting on his knees, his head hanging low. He'd placed the blanket over his head as if hiding.

Lydia crouched down. "How may I help you, sir?" she asked kindly.

His hand shot out from under the blanket and gripped her wrist tight. "Do not make a sound."

She recognized that voice. It dripped with menace.

Huntsford. Oh, God—how did he find her?

Her heart raced, but Lydia admonished herself for feeling anxiety.

Get control. Do not allow this man to frighten or intimidate you any longer.

He squeezed tighter. "I know what you're thinking. How did I find you? It's an interesting tale," Huntsford murmured. "Did it have anything to do with the fact I am being followed?"

Oh, blast it.

Mr. Robins was correct. Huntsford knew.

Harrison had told her of the conversation in the pub two nights past. Frankly, she wouldn't have given John Huntsford that much credit for brains. Since he was so self-absorbed, she imagined he wouldn't notice if anyone watched him. But he had.

Lydia struggled to pull her arm from his tight grip, but he held her firmly. She met his gaze. He wore a false beard.

Why had she not seen the cruel gleam in his eyes before now? Misplaced and misguided love can hide a multitude of warnings.

"It took me wearing a disguise, but I followed the careless bloke to an investigative agency. The tall bastard with the limp and cane—the owner—recently met a couple of men at a pub. One of them, I later discovered, is a marquess. Was it he who hired the agency? I decided to keep watch. Then you emerge from his town house. You've landed on your feet, puss. An heir to a duke?"

His mouth twisted into a lascivious grin. "Have you spread those luscious thighs for him as yet? Used your talented mouth on him? Have you shown him all your wicked ways?"

Lydia's blood boiled. "I'll not be made to feel ashamed of the fact that I enjoy sex. I wish my introduction to it was with any man but you," she snapped, keeping her voice low.

He growled in response, his lips curling. "You lie. You still want me. You're mine. No one else will ever have you. I'll make sure of it, one way or another."

How tempting to throw at him that she was aware of Miss Slickson, but she wouldn't give him the satisfaction nor give away how much they knew of Huntsford and his activities.

"I will never be yours. Not ever again. You are a vile, selfish excuse of a man. Let me go. At. Once." Lydia kept her voice firm, her tone sharp.

It was gratifying to tell him what she thought of him. Any lingering vestiges of feelings for Huntsford dissipated. She felt nothing for him. In truth, she fell out of love with him some months ago.

Not afraid any longer.

"If you don't come with me now, I'll tell the coppers you stole the drugs. I'll inform the head nurse of your debauched ways and how you seduced me to do your will and made me take opium. That your story of an illness is false at its core. Unless you're speaking of the sickness of the soul."

"You're speaking of yourself." Lydia stopped struggling. "How did you know of an illness?"

"I heard someone personally delivered a letter to the head nurse. Curious, I broke into the locked drawer in her desk and read it. It was from you. Quite the tale. It won't hold once I tell all of your true nature."

Lydia yanked his arm toward her and bit his hand until he yelped and released her arm. She had drawn blood.

"Huntsford is here!" she screamed at the top of her lungs.

John's eyes widened, then narrowed as he jumped to his feet.

"Miserable bitch," he seethed.

He knocked her flat and vaulted past her, heading for the short tunnel and the exit. He wasn't that far away from it and could easily escape.

Lydia scrambled to her feet. Already he was becoming lost in the crowd.

"Stop him! Huntsford is here!"

Alas, since most people in the Terminus were probably hiding for one reason or another, no one intervened, whether from authorities or life itself. In fact, they turned away. Lydia scanned the mass of humanity, trying to locate Harrison. All in white, he was easy to spot. But he worked at the opposite end of the cavernous underground area.

Waving her arm to gain his attention, she pointed toward the tunnel. "He's in there!"

Harrison sprinted in that direction, and lifting her skirt, she did the same. Lydia reached it first, stopping when she found a trail of the tattered trousers, coat, and beard on the ground. Huntsford was shedding his disguise as he ran. Underneath, he'd worn his regular clothes. Sly indeed.

A terrible thought entered her mind. Huntsford knew of her connection to Harrison.

A cold fear gripped her tight.

JOHN HUNTSFORD REACHED the boarded entranceway and stopped short. He would have to exit as casually as possible in case someone from that damned detective agency was watching the place. Exhaling, he stepped outside onto Stepney High Street.

A smile curved around his mouth when he saw the crowded streets. A shift change at the nearby boot and shoe factory would be adequate cover.

Pulling his peaked cap out of the pocket of his jacket, he then placed it on his head and pulled it low over his eyes.

He dared not look behind him to see if anyone was in pursuit.

Damn that bitch.

Yelling for help—to whom exactly? The doctor? Just how many men were involved with Lydia?

Bad enough to find a marquess on that list. The Marquess of Tennington met with the ex-copper with the cane. Why? John decided to start surveillance on the Tennington town house.

But today was the first time he was free to do so because of his recent shifts at the hospital. When Lydia had stepped out of the front entrance and into a carriage, he couldn't believe his eyes.

John had flagged a cab, and the driver nearly refused to take him as a customer due to his tattered clothing disguise, but once John had thrust a handful of shillings at him, the driver followed the carriage to the East End to the underground shelter.

Was she Tennington's mistress?

Fury tore through him at the thought of Lydia pleasuring some pampered peer. He furtively glanced about the street and, spotting a cab, waved it down.

"Head to the West End, then back here," he commanded the driver.

"That's a fair piece; I'll need half the fair."

John thrust a pound note into the man's gloved hand. "Drive where I say to drive."

"Yes, sir."

John settled inside and slammed the door. Once the coach lurched forward, he scanned the street, looking for anyone suspicious. This sightseeing route would allow him time to work out a plan and see if anyone followed him.

Damn his pride, he shouldn't have revealed himself to Lydia, but he couldn't help it.

In hindsight, he also shouldn't have told Lydia of his plans to rob the hospital pharmacy.

It was not as if he were addicted to the stuff. He went days without touching opium, primarily when he worked several shifts. But John did enjoy wallowing in his vices on his days off. Foolishly, he believed Lydia felt the same as him until the night of their terrible row.

The stubborn woman had defied him on many fronts. First, by running off without a word, then moments ago in the underground soup kitchen, he commanded her to stay quiet.

How dare she question his authority? His ownership of her?

Yes, he occasionally sought out Fannie Slickson for a quick tumble, and he was temporarily staying with her until he could make other arrangements, but she meant nothing to him—less than nothing.

But Lydia.

John rested his head against the seat cushion. Memories of their erotic adventures flooded his mind. She'd been game for anything. Maybe she had to be coaxed to try the morphine-cocaine mixture—or forced.

What did it matter? Lydia was his to do as he pleased.

Although, John reflected, he shouldn't have hit her that night of the row or forced the needle into her arm against her wishes. He overplayed his hand, perhaps. But he had to make her aware of his authority. It was not to be questioned or denied. The only way to make her understand was to show his domination over her.

Regardless, she would be in his possession once again if he had to follow her to the ends of the earth. No man would touch her, or he would suffer the consequences.

A marquess? Heir to a duke?

John would be playing with fire—especially with a detective agency involved.

To hell with it. He would burn it all down.

As long as after all turned to ash—Lydia was his.

Chapter 18

HARRISON REACHED THE tunnel to find Lydia standing near a pile of clothes. She turned to face him, holding a fake beard.

"Huntsford shed his disguise as he ran," she whispered miserably, "I couldn't catch him."

Sprinting to the entrance, Harrison moved aside the loose boards and stepped onto the sidewalk. A crowd of laborers immediately swallowed him up.

God, he'd never find him in this throng, besides the fact he had no idea what the blackguard looked like except for a vague description from Robins. It could fit any number of men here.

A man in a long coat and a bowler hat approached him. "Is there a problem, my lord?"

"Robins' man?"

Since the terminus was a daily stop in his busy schedule, figuring it out wouldn't be challenging. He would give Robins his due; he figured out he was Doctor Damian. But then Harrison had given the man leave to follow him, telling him of the shelter, not of the fact that he toiled there.

"Yes, my lord. My name is Taylor. Mr. Robins said to keep watch."

"Did you see anyone leave here moments ago?"

"Yes, there were two, both men."

A sprig of hope bloomed. "Did you get a good look at them? What direction are they headed?"

Taylor tugged on his earlobe. "Well, only a fleeting glimpse, my lord. One was older, with gray hair, the other brown hair, a little above average height. Wore a laborers jacket. And he put on a peaked cap. He wasn't acting suspicious, so I continued my surveillance on the entrance."

Harrison exhaled in frustration. "Keep watch. We'll be departing shortly."

"Yes, my lord."

Frustrated and slightly annoyed, Harrison returned to Lydia, taking the beard from her hand. Was this the man who watched them intently at the Red Lion pub? The facial hair was undoubtedly similar.

Damnation. Hell.

"He spoke to you?" Harrison asked.

She nodded. "Huntsford told me plenty. None of it good."

"We will finish up here immediately and return home. We'll talk there." Harrison caressed her pale cheek. "You were brave to bellow out a warning."

Lydia laughed shakily. "A lot of good it did. No one stopped him."

"The people here are worn and weary, and many are hiding. Becoming involved is not an alternative for them."

Lydia nestled her cheek against his palm. "I know, I lived it. I hoped someone would step in."

Forty minutes later, they were sitting in the dining room alone, having just finished a light meal of roast chicken. Lydia relayed to him everything Huntsford had said to her.

The audacity of the man. And completely reckless.

"I am sorry now Sam ever recommended William Robins and his merry band of ex-coppers." He pushed away his near-empty plate in disgust.

"I don't blame Mr. Robins," Lydia replied. "Huntsford is sly and far cleverer than I'd give credit for. But why focus attention on me? Why can't he leave me be?"

"His narcissistic and twisted personality will not allow it. He is obsessed with you and receives a decided thrill controlling you. He misses that. He needs it. It feeds him, gives him power."

Lydia's eyes widened. "My. You are well informed on the subject."

"I assure you I hold none of the same attributes, outside of occasionally slipping into my I-am-an-heir-to-a-duke mask. I studied the German psychiatrist Carl Wilhelm Ideler at university. His thesis is still controversial. He believed passions are important in the origins of mental illness and that certain drives are constantly imbalanced. Not all physicians or scientists subscribe to their being actual diseases of the mind."

"You think Huntsford is insane?"

Harrison blew out a breath of frustration. "The imbalance may have always been there. The drug use no doubt exacerbated it."

Which made him all the more dangerous. During their trip home, an idea had taken root. He might as well mention it to gauge Lydia's reaction.

"You're not out of harm's way, not as long as you stay here. Why not come with me to Hastings? There would be no safer place than at the estate of a duke."

"But the double wedding—"

"You will be attending as my guest."

Lydia shook her head furiously. "Absolutely not. You mentioned it was family only. My presence there would upset those plans and raise speculation about our relationship."

"There will be a few family friends there as well. As I told you, my family is unaware of my secret life. Perhaps I need you as a witness, for I intend to reveal all to them."

Harrison grasped his water goblet and took a drink. "I'm teasing, perhaps a little. But I've had enough of secrets and lies."

He pushed the glass away. "As to our relationship, I will tell my family the truth—for once. I will tell them you have always captured my attention as no woman ever has. That you are under my protection. That we are friends. I'm completely smitten and hope there will be more when you're ready. And that you have a firm hold of my heart."

He met her gaze. "I relinquish it to your care, for I am falling for you, Lydia. I will not deny it any longer."

Lydia blinked rapidly; her lower lip quivered. "Oh, Harrison."

"I assure you I'm not as dull as I outwardly project."

"At this stage, I wouldn't mind a little dull. You are far from that," Lydia whispered. "I've had my fill of arrogant, brooding, possessive men. A generous man of honor? One who selflessly serves his fellowman? Loves his family? Respects women? Oh, I could give my heart to a man such as that."

"If you were to ask it of me," he said in a low, husky tone, "I would tear down the sky."

"What is happening between us?" Lydia whispered.

Harrison smiled wistfully. "Something quite—wonderful. I want to kiss you."

"You do?"

"Yes, standing, facing each other. I'll caress your flushed cheeks, nibble on the pulse point on your neck, slowly move upward and capture your lips, kiss you, take complete possession, taste every inch of your mouth—"

The soft moan that emitted from her was all the invitation he needed. Harrison was out of his chair, bringing her into his crushing embrace, and she softened in his arms.

Then he did as he described: he cupped her face, caressing her cheeks with the pads of his thumbs. He looked into her beautiful blue-green eyes and held nothing back. No more hiding his emotions.

Leaning in, he located that enticing pulse on her neck and nibbled and kissed it until she moaned again.

God, he was aroused, ready to burst into flames. But nothing prepared him for the devastating kiss. Barely touching her lips in the bedroom several nights past had him reeling, but this?

Utterly earth-shattering.

Her tongue tangled with his, increasing the heat between them. Harrison brought her in closer until her ample breasts smashed against his chest, and his arousal pushed against her thigh.

Would she flinch or push him away? To his absolute joy, she flung her arms about his neck, kissing him enthusiastically, pressing against him until a deep-throated growl rumbled up from his chest and escaped the corner of his mouth.

Easy. Regardless of Harrison's rampant desire, he didn't want to overwhelm Lydia.

In slow increments, he reluctantly ended the kiss. "Thank you."

"No, thank you."

Laughing, Harrison gallantly pulled out her chair and then took his seat. Sobering, he caught her gaze. Lydia's eyes were bright, alive.

"It is something wonderful. Can you feel it?" Harrison stated.

She nodded, then a furrow knotted between her brows. "But I cannot attend a family event. Especially one as intimate as a wedding. Surely you see this."

"No, I do not. Besides, there is a place I want to show you. It's not far from my family's estate. It is called The Hornsby and Wollstonecraft Residential Home. It's for those with special needs, mentally and physically. There is no reason you cannot be a nurse there, at least temporarily, until you decide what you wish to do next. It's far enough away from London—and Huntsford. The residence is located in a quiet, tranquil country setting. It will give you time to heal."

Harrison watched her closely as she processed the information. At least she didn't immediately shut the conversation down.

"But it is merely a suggestion. Your decision," Harrison continued. "When I say you're under my protection, it certainly does not mean you're under my thumb. After what you endured with Huntsford, I would never presume to wield such power. We've only known each other for a few weeks. But I feel as if I have known you my entire life."

Damnation, he laid his heart and soul bare. Smitten? No, it was far more intense than that.

His former mistress's wise words entered his mind:

I feel you will follow your brothers down the path of true love with a woman, not of your class. She may even be entirely inappropriate. If you meet such a lady, do not dismiss her. Nor dismiss what you feel.

No, he would not dismiss Lydia or the emotions she evoked in him. *For it is love.*

It filled him with unfettered joy along with a generous helping of dread. He couldn't bear it if she walked away from him. Instinctively, he understood he could not rush Lydia and that she'd suffered during her association with Huntsford, damaged to what depths was anyone's guess. Lydia was struggling with her emotions. Perhaps he'd disclosed too much.

For he had never been in love before.

LYDIA'S INSIDES WERE churning with confusion and overwhelming emotions. This rush of feelings caused her heart to beat so fast it reverberated against her ribcage.

She still hadn't recovered from the kiss, let alone his heartfelt—and heart-melting— confession.

How to reply?

She had no idea what to say. Leaving London was her plan all along, and this would be one way to achieve it. A residential home in a serene country setting? It sounded like the ideal solution.

"Oh. Thank you. I appreciate your honesty regarding your feelings."

"But you cannot address your own at this time."

Harrison wasn't angry. He just spoke matter-of-factly.

"No. Not at this time. But I wish for us to continue to be honest with each other. You can tell me anything. Because I feel as if I've also known you for ages."

"That is a good place to start," Harrison smiled.

Best to keep the conversation focused on the residential home. "Tell me about the home," she asked, returning his smile.

Harrison explained that the Wollstonecrafts, distantly related to the late author, Mary Shelley, collaborated with the Hornsbys on the project about thirty-five years past.

It was the family name for the Earl of Carnstone, and at the time, his granddaughter fell in love with a young man who had not fully matured intellectually and, in some ways, emotionally, hence the desire to found such a home.

What a fascinating story. Lydia had never been to Sussex.

"I've nothing appropriate to wear to a duke's estate."

She was weakening. But reasoning it out, it was a good suggestion. Lydia knew deep in her soul that Harrison would never try to control her like Huntsford.

He smiled broadly. "I know of dressmakers that have certain garments ready to be altered at a moment's notice. I will contact one immediately."

"Excuse me, my lord. Viscount Hawkestone to see you." Youngston announced.

Good heavens, Harrison's servants moved about stealthily. She never heard the butler enter the room.

"My brother, Tremain."

Lydia stood. "Then I will leave—"

"Please stay and meet him. After all, you're accompanying me to his wedding. You are, correct?"

"Yes, I will."

A tall man, leaning heavily on a cane, entered the room. Taller than Harrison, he had raven-black hair and eyes the same mesmerizing shade of silver-gray. And therein was the only similarity to mark them as brothers, at least at first glance.

Harrison strode toward him, and the men clasped each other's lower arm, an odd sort of greeting.

"Sorry to intrude without sending notice," the brother stated. "But I wanted to let you know that I'm leaving for Gransford Manor in the morning. I've hardly seen you the past two weeks except at Parliament."

The viscount's gaze slid to her, and he gave her a thorough assessment. "And I see why you've been pleasantly distracted." His voice was as deep as Harrison's, his expression guarded.

"Tremain, this is Miss Lydia Chesterton. Lydia, my brother, Tremain Hornsby, Viscount Hawkestone."

Lydia held out her hand, and the viscount took it and bent over it, albeit a little stiffly. "A pleasure, Miss Chesterton."

"And you, my lord." Upper-class parlor manners were not something Lydia was used to. "I will leave you both."

"Do not disappear on my account."

The viscount moved to the nearby chair and sat upon it. A grunt left his throat, no doubt from pain, Lydia surmised.

Once she and Harrison took their seats, Youngston stepped forward. Oh. The under-butler had heard her real name. What did it matter now since Huntsford knew where she was staying?

"Shall I bring coffee and tea, my lord? And perhaps cakes?" Youngston asked.

"Tremain? Stay for a cup, at least."

"One cup. And cakes, sure."

"Tea, Youngston, no coffee. Unless Lydia? You would prefer coffee?"

She cleared her throat. "Tea is fine."

Once Youngston left, Harrison turned to his brother.

"Lydia will be accompanying me to Hastings and will be my guest for the weddings," Harrison declared.

The viscount arched an eyebrow in surprise but continued to listen intently about how a man she was involved with endangered her at her previous place of employment.

Lydia noticed Harrison did not mention the Terminus and any activities there. Right. His family wasn't aware as yet.

Harrison only ceased his tale when Youngston entered with the tray, setting it up on a table between them.

"Lydia, would you pour?" Harrison asked.

Her nerve endings sparked at the request. Pouring tea for a marquess and a viscount? Three weeks ago, she battled with a rat in a dirty alley for a bread crust.

Strange how things turned out.

She absently rubbed the top of her hand. The faint scar was a stark reminder of her skirmish with the rodent and her dire situation.

"Why don't you both come with me in the morning? I have a first-class berth on the nine-twenty out of Westminster Station," the viscount suggested.

Harrison seemed to consider it, then shook his head. "Thank you, but no. I will stick to my original departure plans. I believe we will travel by carriage. Besides, I have several obligations to see to before I can leave."

His brother frowned. "If this man is a peril, wouldn't a swift exit from the city be the best option? And no offense to Miss Chesterton, but why expose the family to this danger?"

Lydia's heart stilled. "The viscount is right. I cannot go with you."

"Then it appears I'll not be attending the wedding, for I will not abandon Lydia to the fates," Harrison stated firmly, setting his cup and saucer on the table with a good deal of force.

"What is she to you?" the viscount asked.

Harrison met his brother's inquiring gaze. "She is everything."

The words cut deep, and a lump formed in her throat. Honestly, Lydia was on the verge of tears, and she did not expect this reaction. Harrison all but said that he loved her. Not just falling—but actually in love. His reply deeply moved her, and Lydia's heart soared.

The viscount slid his gaze to Lydia as if assessing if she were worth such an emotionally spoken declaration. Perhaps before meeting Harrison, she would have believed she wasn't. But in the past few weeks, healing had begun, not only of her self-worth but her battered soul. It was a start, though the journey was not complete as yet.

"Then I can delay my departure for two days. Think about it, Harry. There is strength in numbers. Besides your valet, you will also have a man or two from this investigative agency. Better yet, I will send a telegraph to Spence. He is at the manor and will be able to meet us halfway on the journey."

Harrison rubbed his chin and then looked at her. "Lydia?"

How wonderful that Harrison sought her opinion. Not used to it, for Huntsford never had.

Lydia glanced at the brothers, who waited for her response. "I think it a solid plan; I cannot see Huntsford making any move in such a public and enclosed place as a train. But I regret the fact that I'm pulling you all into this. And at such a happy time as a double wedding."

The viscount gave her a brief smile, the first sign of any warmth from him. "The timing may be unfortunate, but if Harry cares for you this intensely, then know that his family, particularly his brothers, will do what we can to assist him. Which in turn means to assist you."

Passing the cup and saucer to the viscount, she returned his smile. "Thank you, my lord."

"Call me Tremain."

"If you will call me Lydia."

They settled in for a relaxing cup of tea. The two brothers discussed the latest bill before Parliament, keeping her in the conversation.

The Married Women's Property Act would receive royal assent in August, be passed, and take effect on the first of January 1883. At last, married women could buy, own, and sell property and keep the earnings. A married woman's legal identity will no longer cease to exist.

Marriage never arose as a topic between her and John, and she was silently grateful. However, he managed to seduce what little money she'd tucked away into his possession. In small drips.

The thought of it angered her afresh—no more admonishments or feeling sorry for herself.

Huntsford and what happened between them was firmly in her past.

Time to forgive herself. Heal, as Harrison had said.

But first to see Huntsford brought to justice. Any justice they could manage, even if they could only use his debt as recourse.

She could not relax or move forward until he was entirely out of her life.

Lydia's gaze slid to Harrison. Nor would she be able to love this brilliant man wholeheartedly as he deserved until all was behind her.

She was already halfway in love with him.

Chapter 19

AFTER TREMAIN DEPARTED, the next twenty-four hours passed in a blur of activity. Harrison made arrangements at the terminus for his absence, instructing the nuns to be a little more aggressive in who could stay at the shelter.

They had been broadminded in their previous decisions but now must insist that those who could find shelter and assistance elsewhere must do it. And the Terminus staff would also now curtail lengths of stay at the facility.

Harrison loathed doing this, but he was short of funds. Besides, Sam located an empty two-story building one street over that could prove to be an ideal location for their clinic/shelter. Best to focus their attention on finding a permanent home.

Speaking of his friend, Sam lounged in the wing chair as Harrison moved about his bed-chamber, selecting the clothing he would take with him to Gransford Manor. Before coming upstairs, he introduced his good friend to Lydia.

"Shouldn't your valet be doing such a chore?" Sam asked.

Sam had just completed his shifts at the hospital and would be taking charge of the terminus while Harrison was at Gransford Manor.

"I like to select my own garments; Gillis will pack them." He turned toward his friend. "I want you to stay here while I'm gone. I've asked you more than once to give up your rented rooms and take up residence here. Think of the money you will save, especially since you're pursuing a young lady of quality. My servants will be at your disposal. Decent meals, a good bed—"

Sam laughed heartily. "Enough. You've convinced me. I paid rent until the end of the month, but I will stay here while you're gone. After that, we will further discuss our living arrangements."

"Good man." Harrison laid some cravats on the bed.

"Preparations have been made with Robins?"

Harrison stopped arranging his clothing and frowned. "I cannot say I have been impressed by his actions regarding this situation."

"William fired the lad who had been followed," Sam interjected. "A stupid mistake of which William is heartily sorry."

"So he said."

"Well, I'm not sorry I recommended him. He *is* skilled, and I've no doubt he will redeem his agency by bringing this situation to a swift and discreet close. The lady will be free of her burden, wait and see."

"One of his men will be traveling with us—Taylor and possibly one other. Robins and the rest will stay behind and pursue Huntsford in the city. He's gone to ground. But from what Lydia has told me of him, I doubt the wayward surgeon will stay hidden for long. He's desperate and will make a move. He's also become reckless." Harrison pulled a revolver from his drawer. "And I will be ready."

Sam's eyes widened. "Since when did you become so fierce?"

"Since the woman I'm falling in love with has been threatened by her previous paramour. I will do all in my power to see her safe. Once the police arrest Huntsford, Lydia will heal and move on with her life. And accept my heart. One thing at a time, however."

"Love? Things are moving at a rapid pace for both of us. I'm surmising the aristo-marriage alliance idea has come to an end?"

Harrison nodded. "It has. I can be a stubborn and misguided sod."

Sam snorted. "No comment from me."

"Upon meeting Lydia, what is your impression? Be truthful. Sizing up people at first contact is one of your talents."

Sam tapped his chin thoughtfully. "She's attractive despite the lingering effects of her illness and homelessness. I saw a genuine warmth in her eyes but also wariness. I don't believe she is cold at heart, but it's obvious she's damaged inside. Will she ever be able to trust again?"

Harrison had told Sam of her background, not all that she revealed, but generalities.

How astute. Therein was the crux of it all.

Would Lydia ever trust him fully and open her heart? Love him completely?

He would settle for no less.

All thoughts of an aristocratic alliance had dissipated into smoke. Another of Harrison's hare-brained ideas. My God, what an idiot he'd been on many topics. He had been too obstinate and self-centered by far. Yes, he did good deeds, but all he seemed concerned with was how it would reflect on him.

No, that is not entirely true.

Harrison was protecting his family. That motive was genuine, at the very least. What blunders he had made. But it was time to own his missteps. Confess it all. And move on to the next phase of his life.

He wanted to share it all with Lydia if she would have him.

"I think you've hit on it. I will give Lydia all the time she needs." He paused, looking toward the closed door. "How much do you think the servants are aware of?"

Sam chuckled. "More than you think. Why not ask them? Why not begin with your household staff if you intend to come out of the shadows?"

Why not, indeed?

Harrison strode to the door, opened it, and found Gillis and Youngston conversing farther along the hall.

"Could you both come in here a moment?"

Harrison motioned for Youngston to close the door. "I have a question to ask you. How much do you know about my night activities?"

The two men exchanged looks. "We know everything, my lord," Youngston replied. "Though not at first. When you took up permanent residence here five years past, you were more careful. Then you started to wear white garments home. Your exhaustion was far deeper than a man engaging in excessive carnal activity."

"I see," Harrison stated. He glanced at Sam, who smiled with amusement.

"Servants talk, my lord," Gillis interjected. "With decided frequency. We were concerned about you, so one night—I followed you. I watched you for two hours, offering medical care to those who most needed it. Well, my lord, naturally, I came back here and reported my findings."

"Naturally," Harrison responded drolly.

"You have your reasons for keeping it quiet, my lord, and we all respect that," Gillis continued. "We decided that night we would do all we could to protect your identity and assist you in any way. Granted, most of it was taking particular care of you, meals, sleep, keeping most household annoyances from bothering you."

"You may not be aware, my lord, but servants from various households do come across each other in shops, pubs, and the like," Youngston interjected. "We perpetuated the tale of your supposed wild exploits. I'm afraid other servants spread the gossip far and wide. Perhaps we were too inventive with your nocturnal adventures. Nonetheless, you have been left alone these past years."

"That I have," Harrison replied softly.

"It has been our distinct honor to serve you, my lord," Youngston said, his voice filled with emotion. "All of us. You're a true gentleman, a man of quality. A man of principle. We will keep your secrets safe for as long as you wish."

Harrison swallowed hard. Hearing these passionately spoken words made him realize that his reasons for secrecy were not all selfish at the core. He did wish to serve his fellow man. Protect his family. Protect those who needed it most, as Gillis said.

"I appreciate it, but it will not remain a secret. There will be changes coming. I'll inform my family of everything when I travel to the manor tomorrow. But never fear, where I go, the staff of this house goes with me, whether it is another residence in London or my estate in Eastbourne. You have my word."

"Thank you, my lord," Youngston said.

"Doctor Kenward will be staying here while I'm gone. Afford him all comforts."

"Absolutely, my lord. We shall see him well taken care of. After all, he has been your good friend and assistant these last years," Youngston replied, bowing in Sam's direction.

"Youngston, we will speak about Miss Chesterton, whom you've known as Miss Best, and her precarious situation later. Gillis, return in fifteen minutes."

They both bowed and departed, closing the door behind them.

"Well, that was interesting," Sam mused.

"I've always trusted them. Otherwise, I would not have arrived home in my medical garments most nights. Nor would they have been working here at the onset if I didn't trust them with my very life."

"They think of you as a champion," Sam stated.

"Bah," Harrison replied dismissively.

But the thought warmed him and gave him confidence for the task ahead. He honestly could not deduce his family's reaction; it could go either way.

Guess he would soon find out.

THE SMALL TRUNK WAS more than half empty. All that was in it were Lydia's few personal possessions and; the second-hand clothing Harrison had provided. He claimed a delivery would be coming from a dressmaker he had contacted.

A maid had been by earlier, taken her measurements, and then sent along to the dress shop. But it was seven o'clock in the evening, and they were departing in the morning. No clothing had arrived as yet.

Her mind drifted to the viscount's visit yesterday afternoon.

"She is everything," Harrison had said.

The look on his face and the emotion in his voice told Lydia that his feelings for her were far more intense than he expressed verbally. Yes, he stated he was falling for her, but Lydia knew it had gone beyond infatuation.

Her emotions tunneled deep as well. Lydia needed time alone, and this residential home may be the answer. But she would not rush into anything.

How much time would she ask for? Six months? A year? More?

Why was she even entertaining the possibility that they could have a future?

He was a marquess, heir to a duke! How often had that refrain tolled like a clanging bell in her mind?

"You are not under my thumb," he had said.

That was true. Not once since meeting Harrison had he ever treated her as Huntsford had.

Huntsford had made her feel powerless. She would never be that woman ever again.

Lydia did not harbor the hope of marriage as it was a long shot at best, considering his status.

But if Harrison wished for an affair, she would not say no. However, Lydia needed a quiet period of reflection before entering into another relationship.

No matter how wonderful the man, or no matter how brief.

Heavens, she was attracted to him, had been from the start.

As for love?

The beginnings of it were there, though it needed nurturing. Or was Lydia merely denying her true feeling for fear of being hurt?

A knock sounded on the door, and Youngston entered carrying five flat boxes, with Harrison carrying three smaller ones directly behind him.

"Your wardrobe has arrived, Miss Chesterton," Youngston announced.

Lydia moved aside the trunk to the opposite side of the bed. "Lay them there, thank you."

With a slight bow, Youngston exited the room.

"I have informed the servants of your real name; I hope you don't mind. I've also informed them of my secret life as Doctor Damian. They already knew of it. And they approve."

"We had a housekeeper-cook growing up, and she was well aware of every aspect of our lives."

"Were you close to her?"

"Yes. I let Mrs. Little go when I moved in with Huntsford and was too ashamed to seek her out once my circumstances changed. Not that she would be at the same address, for she had mentioned moving to Manchester to live with her sister."

The memory was painful, for their parting had not been pleasant. Mrs. Little begged her to reconsider becoming involved with Huntsford, and they argued. If only she'd listened.

Regrets. Lydia accepted and acknowledged them.

Turning her attention to the boxes, she gave Harrison a warm smile. "What is all this?"

"Various gowns and accessories, altered to fit."

"This usually takes weeks—"

"As I said, you have to know which dressmakers have ready-made garments on hand. And being a marquess can hurry an order along. Have a look."

Lydia opened the top box and found a gown of white silk and lace. Her fingers traced across the lacey low-cut neckline. So delicate and lovely.

Harrison opened a smaller box. "It comes with these silk gloves and lace neckerchief or, as the dressmaker called it, a choker."

"White? Isn't that color for a bride to wear, not a guest?"

"Not necessarily," Harrison demurred. "Not that I'm an expert on London fashion. The queen wore white on her wedding day. Some have copied it. But no bride wore white in the four society weddings I have attended in the past ten years. Besides, Mrs. Desfrene thought this gown would be appropriate for the dinner the night before."

She met Harrison's gaze. "There is to be a dinner?"

"Somewhat formal, I imagine, knowing my mother." He moved the box aside and opened another. "This one is for the wedding."

Lydia gasped. She had never seen anything so beautiful. The bodice had light purple velvet, while the rest had a pink and cream roses silk pattern.

Harrison pulled the gown from the box and held it up for inspection.

Oh, my.

There was a purple velvet overlay on the rear of the gown, with puffed layers to accommodate a bustle, which Lydia had never possessed. Nor had she owned anything as lovely as these gowns.

Without thinking, she threw herself against Harrison, curling her arms about his neck.

"Thank you for everything."

Surprised, he laid the gown on the bed and slipped his arms about her waist. His warmth and strength made Lydia weak in the knees. His enticing scent, and—there. No hiding his arousal as he rolled his hips, allowing her to feel the hardness.

"All you have to do is put your arms around me, and I am lost. An immediate and robust reaction. Only you, Lydia. No other women. Ever. Only—you."

She gazed up at him, completely lost in the emotions reflecting in his lovely eyes. "What have I done to deserve you?"

"You are real. You own up to your mistakes, which has given me the courage to own up to my own. You're beautiful, but beyond that, you speak to my heart. We're a perfect fit in all ways. And more."

More? She blinked, almost afraid to ask what he meant, but he captured her lips with his before she could.

Lydia met his kiss, their tongues tangling, and Harrison's hand cupped her breast, his thumb brushing her hard nipple. She gasped, then moaned softly at the rush of passion moving through her.

Huntsford had not killed such feelings. She *could* have a future, whatever it may be, with this glorious man.

Harrison growled, sending a thrill along her spine. Turning her about, he walked her to the wall, then reached under her skirt, laying her leg against his hip.

Yes. There.

His erection lay at her feminine core. Hot kisses trailed across her cheek and neck as he ground against her.

"I yearn to touch you. To have you come apart in my arms," Harrison whispered fiercely. "Slip my fingers through your folds, bring you to completion."

Would it assist in erasing the stain of Huntsford? What if they did only this and nothing else? Would he think her a wanton? This glorious man did so much already to obliterate some of the damage wrought by Huntsford. But more importantly, above all doubts, she yearned to have Harrison touch her.

It had been so long. Was Lydia genuinely ready to move forward?

Taking his hand, she plunged it under her skirt.
"Yes. Touch me."

Chapter 20

HARRISON CAUGHT HER gaze. "I will only do this if you are absolutely certain. As I said, it is up to you. So again, I ask: do you want me to touch you? Make you come? I will do this and nothing more until you say different."

Lydia's eyes were bright; the desire was visible in their depths. Regardless, he would not proceed unless she was sure and until she verbalized her wishes.

"This and nothing more. For now," Lydia whispered.

That was all that he needed to hear. Tunneling under the loose undergarments, he plunged two fingers inside Lydia, and finding her wet, he groaned with satisfaction.

Capturing her mouth with his, Harrison kissed her fiercely. He tangled his tongue about hers, moving in unison with the thrust of his fingers. Finding her nub, Harrison rubbed vigorously, causing her back to arch and her breath to catch. He kept kissing, touching, and bringing them both to the brink in no time.

Trailing his lips across her cheek, he licked the pulse point on her neck, biting gently. Lydia's breathing was uneven, matching his own.

God, he was close.

Then Lydia gave a strangled cry, her muscles inwardly clamping his fingers tight. The pulsating moved through him, basking him in utter bliss. Lydia laid her head against his shoulder in complete exhaustion.

"W-what about you?"

"This was all about you. Your pleasure."

Harrison was ready to spend right this moment, but he meant what he said.

One step at a time. Only at Lydia's invitation.

He would see to his release later. Alone.

He held her, then kissed her flushed cheek. "Rest. Finish your packing. We leave early in the morning."

Harrison turned and left the room, aching. But he would respect her wishes.

Always.

THEY WERE MERE MINUTES from arriving at the train station in Hastings, and Lydia's insides were fluttering nervously. The journey on the train was pleasant enough, the scenery spectacular, and Tremain and Harrison both made her feel at ease.

Harrison decided that the third brother, Spencer, would meet them at the station with some of the duke's men instead of meeting them at the halfway point.

Surely, Huntsford hadn't followed them. Even he couldn't be that clueless. They were quite the entourage with the brothers, Mr. Robins' man, Taylor, valets, and two tall, muscled footmen.

She laid her hand across her roiling stomach. The brothers were speaking of Parliament doings as she continued to stare out the window.

Going to a duke's estate?

Lydia was entirely out of her normal sphere. In days past, she would have been able to handle such a daunting social situation, for her father had brought her up to be confident in dealing with people no matter their standing.

Huntsford destroyed her self-confidence along with many other aspects of her life. She would not allow Huntsford any victory. Time to reclaim her life and her former self. If it took small steps, so be it, as long as she kept moving forward.

The whistle blew as they branched off onto the London, Brighton, and South Coast Railway line.

Harrison laid his hand on hers. "Are you all right?" he asked.

He innately knew when she was distressed. Despite how hard she tried to mask her fears, trepidation must be showing.

"Yes, thank you."

Once the train came to a stop, Lydia became caught up in a whirlwind of activity, the men forming a protective barrier around her as they stood on the platform.

The footmen and valets saw to the luggage while a tall, lean man walked toward them. Tremain and Harrison shouted warm greetings, meaning this must be the youngest brother.

Never had she seen brothers who looked so dissimilar. Spencer had black-brown hair comparable to Harrison, but his eyes were an oceanic blue. Startling, to say the least. He stood at about the same height as Tremain. Harrison took his youngest brother's hand, pulling him into a brief, partial embrace.

Though Spencer stiffened, he patted his brother on the back before they parted. Tremain joined in the welcoming. They were close; it was plain to see.

"Spencer, may I introduce Miss Lydia Chesterton? Lydia, my brother, Professor Hornsby."

He didn't take her hand, nor did he smile, but gave her a slight bow of greeting.

When his eyes locked with hers, she nearly gasped. How hypnotic—and probing. As if he could see clear to her soul.

"Miss Chesterton. A pleasure."

Oh, his voice.

Slightly deeper than Harrison's but appealing nonetheless.

"The same, my lord."

Or should she have addressed him as Professor? She would ask Harrison later.

He escorted them to a large brougham carriage, and the coachman assisted Harrison and Lydia inside. The servants and the luggage traveled in the carriage parked behind. Spencer and Tremain would ride on horses alongside the conveyances.

Once alone, Harrison moved to sit next to her. "Comfortable?"

She smiled at him. "Yes. Perhaps you should tell me the plans for the next few days again."

For me to prepare for them. Steel my spine.

"Mother will have a light tea set up for our arrival. You will meet the rest of the family and the brides-to-be there. There will be no formal dinner tonight. After tea, a servant will show you to your room, a bath drawn if you like, and you will be able to relax the rest of the evening, no doubt a tray brought to your room of whatever you wish."

"Sounds heavenly," she sighed.

"Tomorrow, after a hearty breakfast, we will venture to the residential home so you may have a good inspection and see if it suits your liking." He arched an eyebrow. "Are you sure you don't mind me moving ahead with these plans?"

"I'm merely a guest. Please, continue."

"Tomorrow evening is the pre-wedding dinner. Just family, but formal. The next morning? The double wedding and accompanying breakfast. Again, family and a few close friends. No huge crowds to contend with. A relief for Spence and all of us, I imagine."

"Yes." She caught his gaze and smiled. "And then?"

"We make plans. You will tell me what you want to do next. If you do not like the residential home, I can find similar places for you to inspect."

Harrison laced his fingers through hers. Even through their gloves, there was no mistaking the heat passing between them. The awareness.

Not only passion but deeper emotions. Ones she couldn't acknowledge right now.

"Allow me to thank you once again. You have been incredibly patient with me. Kind. Generous."

"May I kiss you?" Harrison murmured, nuzzling her neck.

So caring for her feelings, precarious situation, frayed nerves, and damaged self-confidence.

"Yes."

This kiss was everything tender yet searing. Not like the fierce one the previous night, but gentle, packing more emotion than she had experienced before.

The kiss no sooner ended when the carriage slowed. After disembarking, everyone became swept up into a tornado of action.

Lydia barely got to inspect the Georgian mansion before she was standing in a room in front of the Duke and Duchess of Gransford. They were a handsome couple, and it was not hard to see where the brothers got their looks.

Introductions were made, and warm greetings exchanged. The duke and duchess were genuinely pleased to see their sons again.

Moments later, two women entered, the brides-to-be, Lydia surmised. After more introductions, servants removed cloaks and coats and brought tea trays into the room.

Everyone was seated on the multiple settees, everyone except Harrison. He stood facing everyone, his hands clasped behind his back.

"I want to tell you all something before we continue with the festivities of this happy event. I have been a fool. A misguided coward who thought I kept secrets to protect the family. I've realized I was doing it more to protect myself—from censure and scrutiny."

"What is it, Son?" The duke asked, his tone soft.

"Since graduating from university, I've been practicing medicine clandestinely. For the past five years, I have been running an underground clinic with Sam Kenward and the nuns of St. Stepney church. Literally underground, in a partially dug and abandoned train tunnel in the East End. I have used my funds near to depletion. That charitable trust you gifted me with is all but gone. I've lied to you for more years than I care to count."

Harrison started pacing back and forth.

"I am no more a rake than I am a courageous man. It's all been lies. Exaggerated by my staff, thinking to protect me. I had no idea they knew of my secret. The rumors were more scandalous than I was aware of. Again, I'm sorry, as it reflects on you all. What does it say that I didn't mind such talk about my supposed wicked ways, but I didn't want my medical mission public? Nothing good, that is for certain."

Harrison paused, turned, and faced his family. Lydia looked at them. The brothers and their ladies were shocked, as was the duke.

The duchess's lower lip trembled, tears welling in her eyes.

"How could you?" his mother whispered. "How could you keep this from us, your parents, your family? At least Tremain told us of his plans before he withdrew from us to be a vicar!"

"Mother—" Tremain began.

"No!" she cried, standing, the tears spilling onto her pale cheeks. "All these years, you allowed us to think you a wastrel. The lies. The betrayal. Did you not think we would support you? We would have! Censure from whom, society? Hang them all! You are an heir to a duke; you can do anything you blasted well please."

The duke stood, slipping an arm about his wife's waist. Leaning in, he whispered, "There, Cath, easy."

Then he looked at his son. "As you can imagine, this is a complete shock. Hurt? Yes, we are. We raised you boys to think and act for yourselves, so I cannot fault you for following your own path. But you should have told us, for your mother is correct. We would have supported you in every way possible. I am gravely disappointed."

"No!" Lydia cried.

Everyone turned to stare at her. This was not her business to interfere, but she couldn't stay quiet.

"Your son is a true hero, not only in my eyes but to all the thousands of people he has assisted over the years. I've seen him at work at the terminus, for that is where we met. I was a nurse, destitute and alone. I had no one and nowhere to go. But I heard of a safe place. Where an angel of mercy doctor treated people cast aside from society."

She gulped as emotions caused her voice to shake. "Harrison saved me. And so many others. He may say he kept it secret to protect himself, but no man who would give much of his soul did so for that reason alone. He wanted to protect you all. I truly believe that. Society is brutal in its judgments. I know."

Lydia looked down at her clasped hands, knowing she had gone too far. The words tumbled out of her mouth before she could halt them.

Harrison stood by her side, laying his hand on her shoulder. "You see why I am falling for this lovely woman?"

She looked up at him and smiled.

"Please forgive me. I humbly apologize for keeping this from you. I will never do such again," Harrison said to his family. Emotion made his tone tremulous.

The duchess hurried toward Harrison and embraced him, and they both stood together for several moments. When they parted, the rest of his family came to him, accepting and forgiving, and Lydia dashed a tear from her cheek.

A loving family. Though it was only her and her father for years, witnessing the love and respect between the Hornsbys had her grieving for what she lost.

Would she ever have it again?

She locked gazes with Harrison, and he gave her such a heated look that her heart skipped a beat. What the future would hold, Lydia had no idea.

Could there be one with Harrison? Dare she hope?

But one thing was sure: witnessing Harrison own up to his mistakes gave her the courage to accept hers and move toward a brighter future.

Chapter 21

HARRISON AWOKE TO FEEL a weight lifted from his heart and soul. He acknowledged his mistakes, asked for forgiveness, and now the next phase of life lay before him. Over breakfast, he'd informed his family of his plans for a permanent clinic shelter, spoken to the earls, and wanted his family involved with the planning.

To their credit, they acted enthusiastically about his plans. And by forgiving him for his thoughtlessness and selfishness. He'd also told of his intention to secure Lydia a position away from London—and danger. Lydia bravely gave a shortened version of her downfall, and her honesty merely opened his family's hearts to her.

Harrison was glad; he wanted them to like her. Accept her.

After a hearty breakfast, they climbed into the carriage to take the short journey to the residential home. Spencer came with them, and Taylor rode a horse alongside the carriage, acting as bodyguard.

Did Robins locate Huntsford? Take him into custody? Harrison could only hope.

"How are your studies going, Spence?"

His brother continued to look out the window. Tremain told him earlier that Spence rarely left Philomena's side, so the fact he volunteered to come with them was a surprise.

"Phil is my life now. I still research, but not like before. She is expecting."

Harrison patted his brother on the knee. "Congratulations to you both!"

"Yes," Lydia smiled. "The very best to you both."

Spence gave them a brief smile. "Justinian and Theodora will be pleased."

"Who?" Lydia asked.

"His Irish wolfhounds. Part of the family, to be sure," Harrison replied, giving her a wink.

"How wonderful," Lydia said. "I've read they're gentle, a perfect breed to have with children."

Spence gave Lydia one of his rare warm smiles. Lydia treated his brother respectfully, and Spence's detached air did not take her aback. It made Harrison love her all the more.

Once they arrived, an attractive, red-haired, middle-aged lady greeted them. She held out her hand.

"Welcome! My name is Megan Hughes-Wollstonecraft Eaton. Quite the mouthful, isn't it? You must be Lydia Chesterton."

Lydia shook her hand. "And this is the Marquess of Tennington and his brother, Professor Hornsby."

After the introductions, Mrs. Eaton slipped her arm through Lydia's.

"I am eager to show you all about the place. This home has been a particular project of mine since I was fifteen. We have expanded. Two more homes are similar to this one, in Somerset and Dover. If this location doesn't suit you, we can place you at one of the others."

"I don't know what to say," Lydia murmured.

"The marquess stated you've had a bad run of late. If someday you wish to tell me the particulars, I am a good listener. A celebrated nurse from St. Thomas's Hospital in London? We would be pleased to have you," Mrs. Eaton smiled warmly. "For as long or as short of a period as you like."

They entered the front hall, and Harrison was struck at the brightness, the large windows, and the cleanliness. Wildflowers adorned every desk and table, giving the atmosphere a pleasant early summer look and smell.

Though the place was named the "Hornsby and Wollstonecraft Residential Home," he had not been here since the opening when he was a child—though he gave a stipend every year to the cause. His mother, in particular, often visited and kept the family informed of developments, improvements, and how the foundation put their monetary contributions to good use.

"Not all of our staff lives on the premises, so a few rooms are vacant. Here is the one I thought you would like." Mrs. Eaton stepped aside to allow Lydia to enter.

"Better than asylums," Spencer interjected as he glanced about his surroundings.

To think doctors had recommended that Spencer be sent to one. Thank God his father had the foresight to refuse.

"Much better indeed, my lord," Mrs. Eaton replied. "Our patients are treated humanely, with respect and care specific to each individual case."

Harrison had to admit the room was a good size. It had a small fireplace, a round table and two chairs in the corner, an armchair by the fire, and a large bed with an accompanying dresser and wardrobe. Paintings of ocean waves adorned the wall, decorated in a light sand shade.

"A water closet, basin, and small tub are in the rear. We have modern plumbing. Behind that is a small storage area for your personal use. Three doors down is the staff kitchen, where you can heat water for a cup of tea, make a sandwich, and the like, outside the full meals served in the dining room. Would you like to look around?"

Mrs. Eaton walked over to the window and pulled the curtains aside. It was a glass door leading out into a garden area.

"Oh, how beautiful," Lydia gasped.

"Why not stroll about the flowers and shrubs while I take the marquess and the professor to the office? Then we will continue with the tour."

"Thank you, I would like that very much."

Harrison's heart stuttered in his chest. Lydia liked this place; he could tell. It was a serene environment for her to continue to recover. And be about her nursing career once again. Harrison took one last look at her as he headed into the hallway.

There was no doubt of it.

He loved her more than life itself.

All he wanted was for her to get well. Regain her sense of worth.

And, maybe someday, love him in return.

LYDIA SIGHED AS SHE stepped onto the stone path. Already she decided to take a position here, even without the rest of the tour. Lydia knew enough at first glance that this was a well-run home, clean, fresh, and bright. The few patients she'd seen were kept busy with various activities. They were well cared for. Loved. Treated with dignity. Isn't that all anyone ever wanted, no matter the circumstances?

Removing her gloves and tucking them in her cloak pocket, she trailed the tips of her fingers along the top of a manicured shrub. Without warning, a rough hand clamped against her mouth.

"Keep quiet. You're coming with me. Where you belong," a foul breath hissed in Lydia's ear.

Huntsford! Do not panic. Keep your wits. Stall him from leaving, for Harrison and his brother will return anytime.

The gardens were not in a courtyard but opened up into the rear of the home. That must be how he accessed the property.

My God, he followed them here? From London?

"If I release my hand, you will not scream, correct?"

She gave a quick nod. When Huntsford moved his hand, a revolver jabbed into her side. Lydia turned slightly, catching a glimpse of his face. He looked disheveled; his pupils dilated. Of course, he was under the influence.

"Why can't you leave me be?" she whispered. "Why do this? You're not thinking straight. It's the opium, the morphine; it has twisted you beyond recognition."

He'd always been possessive. At first, Lydia had reveled in the attention, but it soon got out of hand with the increase in his drug use, like now.

"I am not your possession to do with as you please. Our relationship turned toxic—ruined, John, beyond all hope. You know this. I'm trying to get my life back on track; I suggest you do the same. Please, I beg you."

He snorted. "A pretty speech, acting like you care a damn. Why do this? Because you are *mine*. No bloody marquess is going to take you from me."

Huntsford pulled her against him, and his erection prodded her back. Lydia's insides tumbled with revulsion.

"Remember how it was between us?" he continued. "We can have that again. I still have drugs left from the theft. We can play as we did before, me rubbing the powder on you while I pound inside—"

"Release her at once, Huntsford!"

It was Harrison and his brother.

Relief covered her at the sight of them. Mrs. Eaton looked on in shock. It was then she noticed Harrison had a revolver of his own.

Oh, no!

The last thing she wanted was for Harrison to be in danger his brother, too.

Huntsford moved the barrel of the gun to her temple. "Back away, my lords. And Tennington, lower your pistol, or I may have a fatal accident with my own," he spat. "We'll be leaving now. You're coming with me, aren't you, love?"

"Y-yes. Whatever you want. I will come with you. Don't hurt anyone."

Huntsford backed up several steps, yanking Lydia along with him. Her mind raced.

Kick his leg? Elbow his guts? Could she move swiftly enough to escape being shot? Huntsford was capable of it. Could she scramble far enough away for Harrison to take a clear shot?

With that thought barely formed, a thunderous bang exploded.

Lydia thought: *that's it, it's the end.*

But it wasn't her that screamed. Or Harrison.

Huntsford fell to his knees, dropping the revolver, then held onto his left shoulder, blood trickling between fingers.

"An excellent shot, Robins. Well done," Harrison said.

Lydia whirled about to see Mr. Robins, Taylor, and two other men with weapons drawn.

"We followed him here, my lord," Mr. Robins said. He held up a carpet bag. "What remains from the St. Thomas theft. Found it in his rented room in Hastings. We'll take him into custody. Put him up at the local jail until we can transport him to London."

"Excellent, Robins," Harrison nodded. "Well done."

Taylor hurried in and gathered up Huntsford's firearm.

"Huntsford will need medical care, for he is under the influence," Lydia murmured. Then she cleared her throat and spoke louder. "The withdrawal from the opium."

Why she even cared about Huntsford's fate—well, she was a nurse.

"Mrs. Eaton, is there a dispensary here? Do you have cocaine?" Harrison asked.

Mrs. Eaton stepped forward, shock still registering on her face.

Huntsford could have spoiled Lydia's chances of working here. For what Huntsford put her through, she should let the miserable man shiver and vomit in a damp prison cell.

"Yes, there is. And we do have it." Mrs. Eaton replied.

"Robins, I'll gather the drug and follow you into Hastings. It will assist in treating the worst of his withdrawal symptoms," Harrison interjected.

Robins nodded as he pulled Huntsford to his feet.

Lydia's ears were ringing from the gunshot, but she was surprisingly serene, at least calmer than she thought she would be. Unless she was in shock. Be damned if she would go to pieces. Not anymore.

A wave of relief covered her. It was over. She could truly move on with her life.

Harrison gathered her into his arms. "If anything happened to you, I would have ceased to breathe."

One gasping sob escaped, but she kept her tears in check. And she held on to this magnificent man for dear life.

WHAT A DAY. DESPITE disturbing the peace of the residential home, Mrs. Eaton insisted the position was still open if Lydia wanted it. She accepted wholeheartedly. After the double wedding, she would move into the room and begin her work.

Once they returned to Gransford Manor, the explanation to Harrison's family was the next hurdle to overcome. The duchess insisted on tea and cakes and gave her a hug for good measure.

After a hot bath and a rest, she joined the family for dinner. Despite the circumstances, the food was enjoyable, and the conversation was lively. Philomena and Eliza were particularly empathetic, for they had similar tales. The family welcomed her as one of them, and she was grateful.

Now standing on the balcony looking up at the stars, she allowed herself a quivering smile.

Right now, at this moment, was a new beginning.

Strong arms encircled her waist from behind, pulling her close. With a contented sigh, she leaned her head back, resting against the warmth and strength of Harrison.

"Have I told you how beautiful you look in this white gown?" he murmured. "How it lovingly caresses your curves. You are stunning, my Lydia."

She closed her eyes, reveling in the closeness, the feel of his hard body molded against hers. The softness of his beard rubbed against her neck—the heat of his passionately spoken words.

"I want nothing more than to take you upstairs to my bed and make love to you all night. But only at your invitation. When you're ready." He kissed her neck, then tugged playfully on her earlobe. "And I should not have said that aloud."

Lydia turned in his arms, clasping his cheeks, meeting his gaze. "I want that. I do. I love the passionate way you talk about what you want. But I need time. I will be starting my new position tomorrow. I have a favor to ask. When you have done so much for me already."

"What is it?"

"That we have had no contact for a while. Allow me to heal. Recover. Think about what I want next."

She requested a great deal. In effect, she asked Harrison to wait for her until she was ready to enter into a relationship, whatever that would entail. Presumptuous of her, considering they hadn't discussed mutual love in any meaningful way. Perhaps all he wished for was an affair.

"How long a period? I will agree to whatever you say."

So understanding.

"Shall we say three months from today? In that time, you can plan your new clinic."

"September 20th?"

"Yes."

"On that date, you will inform me if you want me—or not. I spoke the truth earlier; I am falling for you. I will not say the words, for I do not want to put undue pressure on you. But I will do as you ask. Know this: on the 20th, I'll tell you everything in my heart. Is that acceptable to you?"

Lydia kissed his cheek. "The fact you even ask permission or ask for my opinion has me falling for *you*. It is fine if you allow me to tell you what's in *my* heart."

He touched her forehead with his. "You were brave this afternoon. You asked that Huntsford be cared for; it speaks of your generous heart."

"Did you see him?" she whispered.

"For a moment. I administered the drug. Showed Robins how to do so. They will be heading to London tomorrow. We sent a telegraph to L Division in Lambeth, and the police awaited his arrival. He'll be charged with theft, attempted kidnapping, bodily harm to another, and anything else they can come up with. Too bad criminal transport is not still in effect. Sending Huntsford to New South Wales is appealing indeed."

"A tragic ending, nonetheless. I no longer feel anything for Huntsford except pity. I haven't felt anything for him for a long time."

Harrison kissed her cheek. "I am gratified to hear it. Shall we rejoin the family?"

Lydia nodded, taking his arm. She loved him. And if all went well the next three months, she would tell him what was in her heart. For it was bursting with happiness.

Whatever the future would bring, she would embrace it—wholeheartedly.

Chapter 22

"I NOW PRONOUNCE YOU man and wife and man and wife," the vicar stated.

Applause broke out in the parlor as Tremain and Spencer thoroughly kissed their new brides. The small congregation of family and close friends rushed forward to offer their hearty congratulations.

Harrison stayed put, his gaze never wavering from Lydia. She did the same. It was as if they had said the vows as well, made an unspoken commitment.

God, how he ached for her, but not only physically. He wanted to share his life with her—all aspects. Duty pales in comparison to finding the love of your life. Hang society and their judgment on all counts. If only he'd come to that realization earlier.

He was not a perfect man.

He made monumental mistakes that caused pain to others. It would take time for him to forgive himself. Three months apart would put much in perspective. And he would be busy with the new clinic.

The future looked bright for the Hornsby brothers—the entire family.

A small hand slipped into his. "Come, Uncle! There will be chocolate cake," Drew Payne smiled. "And shortbread with icing and small ginger biscuits."

He squeezed the lad's hand. Drew would soon have the Hornsby name, as Tremain and Eliza had already put the legal aspect in motion.

"I believe there is more to eat besides treats."

He scrunched up his nose. "Eggs and ham? I'd rather have cake."

"So would I, lad. So would I." Harrison laughed, holding out his free hand in Lydia's direction.

Lydia took it, and the three of them headed toward the newly married and happy couples.

The future looked bright indeed.

THREE MONTHS LATER

"NURSE LYDIA! LOOK AT the sun I painted!"

Lydia took the proffered paper and admired it. "It is a brilliant sun, Sophia." Sophia was one of the sweetest girls she had ever met. Only Sophia was not a girl but a young lady of twenty-six. She handed the paper back to her. "You've taken your medicine? Feeling better?"

"Yes, I did. My tummy is better, thank you."

Lydia patted Sophia's shoulder and moved to the young boy sitting opposite. He was rocking slightly but using wooden building blocks to build a fort.

"I am going to feel your forehead, William, all right?"

He quickly nodded, and Lydia laid her palm flat against it.

"Not as hot as before. You are getting well."

He nodded again, and Lydia smiled at him. About to move to a nearby table, one of the volunteers came to the door.

"Nurse Chesterton, there is someone to see you."

Her heart skipped a beat, then another. She had no sleep the night before, for today was September 20th. Harrison was here.

"Lord Tennington is waiting in your room."

"Thank you."

She hurried past, practically running along the corridor. As she moved closer to her room, she slowed her pace.

There Harrison stood, looking out through the glass door. She nearly wept from the familiar sight of his broad shoulders.

He turned and smiled. "Good afternoon, Lydia."

How she yearned to embrace him. What stopped her? The absence of three months caused them to be tentative, unsure about what to do or say next.

"Hello, Harrison," she whispered.

"You look well. Rested. Content."

"I am, thank you. And you are hale and hearty. Rested."

He'd put on a couple of healthy pounds. So had Lydia. Neither of them looked as weary.

Harrison tossed his gloves inside his hat and placed them on the nearby table.

"You've enjoyed your time here?"

"I have, very much."

He took a couple of steps closer. "The plans for the clinic have steamed ahead. Thanks to my father and brothers, we've more contributors than we could have hoped for. We bought the building next door to expand the clinic. Renovations have already begun."

"I am so pleased to hear it."

"To abruptly change the subject, we barely knew each other a month before we parted."

"That is true."

"I feel as if I have known you far longer. All my life." With a smile, he moved a little closer. "I love you, Lydia—with every part of heart and soul. These three months apart were absolute agony."

"For me as well," she replied softly.

"Think of the future we could have."

"Future? As to what?" she whispered.

"You would be my partner in all things. My equal. My lover, my friend."

"A long-term affair?"

Harrison scoffed. "No, my dearest. As my wife. If you will have me."

"Of course, I will have you," her voice tremulous. "For the rest of my life. What will I be?"

"A marchioness. Lady Tennington. Someday—I hope long into the future—the Duchess of Gransford. But that is what society will see. To me, you will be my entire world. Lydia Chesterton. You will always be your own woman. You will never lose your identity. Not to me or to anyone who counts. I would never expect you to be any less than you are. Equal partners, my love. My promise to you. Does entering this privileged but pompous world give you pause?"

Lydia had given it plenty of thought these past months, weighing the pros and cons.

"I deserve to be happy, to love unconditionally, as do you, Harrison. No one, ever again, will make me doubt my worth. What do class and society matter if we are together?"

"I want us to marry as soon as we can arrange it. If you agree, I said I would lay everything bare, and I have." He opened his arms. "Tell me again that you feel the same. That you want to share our lives. I love you with my whole heart."

A tear welled in her eyes. Without hesitating, she rushed into Harrison's arms. She was home. It was where she felt safe, warm, and cherished.

"I love you too. So much."

Cupping her cheeks, he kissed her. A gentle nibbling of her lips, then it swiftly turned into searing passion. Lydia returned it happily.

He pulled back a little. "And marriage? Our lives together?"

"I want it all, everything you said and more. Yes, I will marry you."

He kissed her again. "I want you. Come away with me. We'll get a room somewhere." Then he gazed into her eyes. "Or we can wait. Your call, my love."

Lydia stepped out of his embrace and strolled to the door. She held up a sign that said: Do Not Disturb.

"See this? The staff uses it to ensure quiet time. We can use it now, but we must be quick and quiet. You might as well know this about me. I can be bold."

Harrison's eyes narrowed, his look sleepily sensual. "I am counting on it."

"How soon can we wed?"

Harrison smiled, patting his coat pocket. "There are times being part of the privileged class has its benefits. Perhaps my arrogance shows, thinking you would agree to marry me."

"But?" she asked hopefully.

"I've secured a special license on the outside chance you agreed to marry me."

Laughing, Lydia ran to his arms. He held on tight and spun her around.

He kissed her, then said, "Whatever you want to do, Lydia, I will comply happily. Do you want to stay working here? It can be arranged. Do you want to assist me with the planning and running of the clinic? We can volunteer whenever we like. Hire whom we wish. We can do all this and raise a family besides. We can do anything we put our minds to. What do you think?"

Lydia brushed aside a lock of hair that fell over his eyes. "I would love to help you plan the clinic. I also want to keep my hand in here. We can plan visits to Gransford Manor, and I can also volunteer here."

"Done. I have a country place by the sea, about thirty miles south of here near Eastbourne. A place, I believe, we will use for the marriage—if you agree. We can make it our country home. Close enough to keep a hand in whatever we plan. I cannot wait to begin."

"Our life?"

Harrison nuzzled her neck. "No, love. Our adventure."

AND THREE DAYS LATER, at Eastbourne

AS THE WEDDING GUESTS departed, Harrison and Lydia finally found themselves alone. Turning the key in the door, Lydia turned to face her husband.

"How long I have waited for us to be alone."

"Have you, my lady?"

"Oh. My lady. I like that. Remember what I said about quick and quiet?"

A growl emitted from deep in his chest. "Quick, I can do, at least at the start. We have the rest of the afternoon and the entire evening before us. Quiet? Absolutely not. This manor house is our place; make as much noise as you wish, love."

Harrison pulled off his coat and tossed it aside. Then he unbuttoned his waistcoat and threw it over his shoulder.

"We will not be emerging from these rooms for days."

"I like the sound of that."

Lydia met Harrison in the middle of the room. Laying her hands flat against his chest, she reveled in the warmth of his hard body. Trailing her fingers across the pearl buttons of his shirt, she slowly pushed them through the holes.

"I hate to mention his name, but we must discuss Huntsford. I always made certain he was sheathed."

"Good. As you know, my wicked reputation is mostly counterfeit. I only visited my mistress every few months or so. The association ended before I met you. I've been with no one since. I also used sheaths. Do you wish me to use them here?" he murmured.

Lydia reached under her skirt and pushed down petticoats and drawers, kicking them aside. Giving Harrison a sensual smile, she gave him a gentle shove into the leather chair and climbed into his lap, her knees resting on either side of his hips. She pulled up her skirt as she kissed him.

"Not at all. We wish to start a family; what better time than tonight?"

"What better time, indeed? I will spend the rest of the autumn paying exclusive attention to you—and for the rest of our lives. We will do whatever you wish. Rides in the carriage. Dinner. Theater. We can stay here and then travel to London. You only have to say the word."

"Sounds wonderful."

She traced the fullness of his lips with the tip of her finger. Lydia ground against his arousal.

Harrison groaned.

"So, quick?" she teased.

"Bloody hell, yes," he murmured seductively. "I'm ready to shatter at your slightest touch, so quick will be no hardship."

He fumbled with the fall of his trousers, pulling out his stiff shaft. Reaching under her gown, she grasped it, squeezing it firmly.

Lydia wanted this and wanted Harrison—her husband. Positioning herself, she lowered slowly, taking him deep.

Harrison threw his head back, the cords in his neck pulled tautly.

"Damnation. If only we could stay like this forever," Harrison moaned.

Lydia began to move, a rocking motion soon joined by Harrison sitting forward and thrusting upward in concert with her. They kissed, and the pace quickened, both anxious to savor every sizzling sensation.

Oh. There. Perfect.

Her breath expelled in short bursts. Then the climax slammed her hard, and Harrison caught her cry of ecstasy with his mouth, kissing her deeply. Moments later, he followed with a shuddering release of his own. They held each other close, quaking from their releases.

"It will only get better if possible," he murmured.

They embraced as their breathing regulated.

Harrison laid hot kisses along her low neckline. She was wearing the white lace gown he'd bought her months earlier.

"If I didn't adore you in this gown so much, I would tear it from you," he growled as he reached behind her to unlace and loosen the bodice.

Oh, yes. The thought thrilled Lydia to her toes.

He pulled down the neckline, exposing her breasts. Harrison laved his tongue around her hard nipples, sucking, caressing, and wringing cries of ecstasy from her.

Slipping his hands under her rear, he stood, walking them toward the bed. He undressed her once he lowered her, and her slippered toes touched the floor. He then stood back to admire her.

"Stunning. You are beautiful."

Smiling and basking in his praise, Lydia did the same to Harrison. Slipping off his shirt. Removing his trousers, socks, shoes, and drawers.

Oh. Harrison was well put together—in every way.

Their gazes locked, the yearning a living entity.

Once on the bed, Harrison pulled her close, as they had that night she'd curled up next to him for comforting warmth. His erection was not hard to miss. Rolling her hips, she rubbed her rear end against it, eliciting one of his husky groans.

Lacing his fingers through hers, he whispered, "Lay your leg across my hip."

Lydia no sooner did as he asked when he entered her with a swift slide.

"I love the feel of you inside me," she moaned.

Harrison quickened the pace. "Good," he rasped. "For I may never leave."

They laughed and loved and did so for the rest of their lives.

Epilogue

AUGUST 1892

Ten years later

Harrison had much to reflect on since becoming the Duke of Gransford four months past. The family still grieved the loss of his father, a formidable presence in all their lives, but they came together today to celebrate a happy occasion: the birth and baptism of his and Lydia's third child, a girl they named Myra Ann.

This child was not expected but welcomed all the more because of it. There were two protective older brothers to keep watch, the eldest, Ashley, aged nine, and, now, the Marquess of Tennington, and Duncan, age seven.

Happy voices filled the parlor.

Harrison raised his glass in Sam Kenward's direction. His good friend was here with his wife, Adelia Wollstonecraft. Also with them was their daughter, Patricia, and young son, Aidan, named after Adelia's father, the Earl of Carnstone.

Sam was the managing director of the Hornsby Free Clinic, which now boasted four locations in Greater London. They wanted to expand to smaller outlying districts, specifically those in particular need.

Spencer stood nearby with Philomena and their daughter, Lorene. Tremain and Eliza sat with the dowager duchess, bravely holding up despite losing her beloved husband.

His mother was happily occupied with Tremain's three children, Covina, Clarisse, and son, Hayden.

Standing with Sam was Tremain and Eliza's adopted son, Drew, on break from his medical studies at Cambridge. He'd informed Harrison that he wanted to work at one of the clinics for a few years. Harrison could not be prouder. As was the rest of the family.

The Hornsby family has grown this past decade. The Hornsby brothers chose life and love partners that could not be more removed from accepted society.

And they didn't care a whit.

Let the gossips speculate, turn their noses up. Harrison could not imagine life without Lydia. His duchess. It would have been a hollow and lonely existence without her.

Spencer and Tremain would no doubt say the same about their loves.

Harrison placed his whiskey glass on the table and strode toward his wife, sitting on the settee, holding their infant daughter. She glowed with happiness. He loved her more each day. Harrison told her once he would tear down the sky for her.

Today? He would tear down the moon and stars as well.

Author's Note

COCAINE WAS RECOGNIZED by the British medical community in 1884 as an effective treatment as an anesthetic in surgery and used in several other ways, including treating opium and morphine addiction. Since my story took place in 1882, I took a little creative license regarding the wide availability. Cocaine did not become illegal in Britain until the Dangerous Drugs Act passed Parliament in 1920.

Society thought of doctors in the Victorian era as decidedly middle class. Upper-class people (women could study medicine as of 1876) could study medicine but were frowned upon from practicing it. In my research, I found a few physicians who became part of the peerage or just below it *after* they practiced medicine. But I discovered none who started in the peerage, then became a physician. So Harrison's profession is fictional, to be sure.

The 7th Earl of Shaftsbury was an actual figure, a prominent force in Parliament who championed the underprivileged. A philanthropist and social reformer, he had a hand crafting many child labor and factory reforms and in education. He was known as the "poor man's earl."

The Wollstonecrafts mentioned in this story are fictional characters, and you can find their tales (that take place about thirty-eight years before this trilogy) at digital book retailers. The three-book series is called The *Men of Wollstonecraft Hall.* Read a sneak peek of book one, *Marriage with a Proper Stranger*, in the pages ahead.

More Books by Karyn Gerrard

~HISTORICAL~

The Spinster and Mr. Glover-The Revised Edition (Book #1 Blind Cupid Series)

The Governess and the Beast (Book #2 Blind Cupid Series)

The Copper and the Madam (Book #3 Blind Cupid Series)

Protecting the Duke (The Rakes of St. Regent's Park #1)

The Baron and the Mistress-Revised Edition (The Rakes of St. Regent's Park #2)

Knight of Christmas (The Rakes of St. Regent's Park #3)

Duke of Pain (The Rakes of St. Regent's Park #4)

Bold Seduction (of Professor Hornsby) (Book #1 Hornsby Brothers Series)

The Vicar's Frozen Heart (Book #2 Hornsby Brothers Series)

Marquess of Secrets (Book #3 Hornsby Brothers Series)

Beloved Monster (Book #1 The Ravenswood Chronicles)

Beloved Beast (Book #2 The Ravenswood Chronicles)

Marriage with a Proper Stranger (Book #1 Men of Wollstonecraft Hall Series)

Scandal with a Sinful Scot (Book #2 Men of Wollstonecraft Hall Series)

Love with a Notorious Rake (Book #3 Men of Wollstonecraft Hall Series)

The Not So Perfect Duke (The Rakes of St. Regent's Park #5)

The Viscount of Shadows (The Rakes of St. regent's Park #6) Coming Soon!

~Contemporary~

My Highlander Cover Model (Heroes of Time Travel Anthology Series #1)

Timeless Heart (Heroes of Time Travel Anthology Series #2)

My Wicked Soul (It's Never too Late for Love Anthology Series #1)

That Christmas Feeling (It's Never too Late for Love Anthology Series #2)

Wild Pitch

He's the Wicked Bad (Wicked Men of Rockland City #1)

His Wicked Celtic Kiss (Wicked Men of Rockland City #2)

His Wicked Cold Heart (Wicked Men of Rockland City #3) coming soon!

Author Biography

A MULTI-PUBLISHED AUTHOR from Eastern Canada, Karyn Gerrard loves to write sensual historical and contemporary romances. Tortured heroes are an absolute must.

Karyn's been happily married for a long time to her own hero. His encouragement and loving support keep her moving forward.

To learn more about Karyn and her books: Visit: http://www.karyngerrard.com/

Also, visit her on Facebook, Twitter, Pinterest, Instagram, and Bookbub.

"Looking for a swoon-worthy read? You can't go wrong with the lovely and emotional romances from Karyn Gerrard." ~**Vanessa Kelly, USA Today Bestselling author**

"Karyn Gerrard writes very enjoyable, richly textured historical romances." ~**Kate Pearce, New York Times and USA Today Bestselling author**

Sneak Peek: Marriage with a Proper Stranger

(Book #1 Men of Wollstonecraft Hall) by Karyn Gerrard

Prologue

WOLLSTONECRAFT HALL, Kent
Autumn, 1831

Taking a stroll through a gloomy graveyard was the last thing thirteen-year-old Riordan wished to do on this dismal, overcast autumn day. But he and his twin brother, Aidan, followed dutifully behind their grandfather as he led them to the private area on the edge of the vast estate of Wollstonecraft Hall.

Ravens cawed loudly overhead as they swooped and circled above the rows of tombstones. Gnarled trees stood around the perimeter of the cemetery, as if guarding the dead. Riordan swore he could see screaming faces in the patterns of the bark. A breeze rustled the remaining leaves, creating an eerie sound, causing a chill to curl about Riordan's spine. Aidan, however, was not affected by their gothic surroundings; he gave Riordan a shove, almost knocking him from his feet.

"Stop it," Riordan whispered fiercely.

Aidan gave him a smug smile and shoved him again. It was tempting to wrestle his annoying brother to the ground, but he decided against it when their grandfather stopped before a polished marble tombstone. "It is time you lads learned of the curse."

That brought Riordan up short. He'd heard whisperings from other boys in town and between the servants, but had never given the story another thought. To him, it was a fairy tale, and he was far too old for fairy tales.

"See all these graves? They belong to women who dared to love the men of Wollstonecraft Hall. Many of the men married young, had their first child before the age of twenty, and all buried their wives only a few years into their marriages. Most of the unfortunate women have died in childbirth. Generations of women who either married or were born into the family. Your own mother survived your birth only to succumb four years later to a heart ailment called carditis." His grandfather laid a hand on top of the stone.

Fiona Fannon Black Wollstonecraft.

Riordan and Aidan's Irish mother. Sadly, he had no memories of her. He glanced at his brother; Aidan's expression was as serious as his own. He turned his attention to their grandfather.

"She was a rare beauty, your mother. Your father met her while on a business trip. He'd gone to meet with her father, a rich Irish merchant, as we wished to expand trade. At least, as far as the Corn Laws would allow." This was the most Riordan had ever heard about his mother and her family—his father refused to speak of her. "A whirlwind romance. I advised him before he left to guard his heart. But he did not listen to me."

"Why is it we've never met our Irish grandfather?" Aidan asked.

"Ah. He was quite distraught when informed of your mother's death—blamed your father. He claimed he wanted nothing to do with him or his sons. It's his loss that he does not wish to know you boys." He pointed to a tombstone in the aisle behind them. Riordan and Aidan turned and found a crow perched on the stone, giving them a defiant look. It was a disturbing vision, and it caused another shiver to trickle through him.

"There rests my first wife, your grandmother, Lady Patricia Ackerly, daughter to the Earl of Clapham. Not exactly a love match, but a solid one in society's eyes. She gave me a fine son, your father. However, she never recovered from the trauma of his birth, contracted a bed fever, and died a month later. I swore my next wife would be of heartier stock. I would defy the Wollstonecraft curse and swiftly end it."

Their grandfather moved along the row and laid his hand on top of another gravestone. A wistful sigh escaped his throat.

Moira Mackinnon Wollstonecraft

Uncle Garrett's Scottish mother. "God, how I loved Moira," he whispered mournfully. "But it wasn't enough to shield her from the curse."

Riordan did not like the sounds of this. He and Aidan exchanged worried looks.

"I met Moira in Edinburgh about twelve years after your grandmother died. She was the epitome of a bonnie lass, with her fiery red hair and passionate nature. Does your father ever speak of her?"

Riordan nodded. "He said he remembered her always smiling."

"She embraced this family. Became a mother to Julian. She always had a song in her heart. When Garrett was born, my happiness was complete. I didn't give a hang what society thought about my choice of bride. For once in my life, I was content and in love. At peace." A lone tear trickled down his cheek. "But it was not to be," he whispered. "I wish you could have known her. She died when Garrett was five years of age. The year before you lads were born."

"I thought the curse was broken if a Wollstonecraft man found true love?" Aidan asked. It was the first Riordan had heard of this. How did Aidan know about it?

Their grandfather barked out a cynical laugh. "Apparently not, for what I had with Moira was all that and more. Your father thought he'd found it. Yet here our wives lay, taken from us far too young. The doctor claims Moira died of a cancer that lay dormant for years, long before we met. Who is to know what to believe?" He shook his head.

"I dismissed the curse and refused to allow it to rule my life. Your Uncle Garrett needed a mother. Three years later, I remarried. A complete miscalculation, as we were not compatible. Yet I managed to get her with child the three or four times I visited her cold bed."

Riordan was not used to such frank talk from his grandfather, and his cheeks flushed with embarrassment. A wave of apprehension rolled through him.

"She died giving birth to a girl, who died three weeks later. They are buried together there." He pointed to a small stone farther along the row. "Heed me, lads. The proof is before you. Let no female close, for it will end in tragedy. Ultimately, it will be your decision to involve yourself with a young woman when you're older, but you would be better off guarding your heart. Do you understand?"

"Yes, Grandfather," they answered in unison.

All at once, the dead-leafed trees appeared skeletal and more terrifying. Riordan couldn't suppress the shiver that ran through him. A terrible sense of foreboding took hold. Death, tragedy. All of this occurred before he was born, or he was too young to have it impact him. But it did now. His family was cursed. He was cursed. He would not forget this day.

Not ever.

Chapter 1

Wollstonecraft Hall, Kent
August 1844

GROWING UP IN AN ANCIENT, medieval hall filled with powerful men had not been without its issues, mainly when tragedy and loss hung over the place like a heavy, melancholy mist on the moors. Today, however, Riordan was ready to embark on a new chapter of his young life.

Since sleep had been sporadic the previous night, he arrived in the dining room for breakfast and the first Monday-of-the-month family meeting before the rest of his family. Rubbing his hands together to elicit a little warmth as he entered the room, the enticing aromas of bacon, ham, and coffee filled his senses. Murmuring "good morning" to the phalanx of footmen standing by, Riordan lifted the covers of the silver chafing dishes and commenced loading his plate with food.

Martin, the butler, already well-versed in Riordan's beverage preference, prepared his tea the way he liked it, with two teaspoons of sugar and the milk added first. He set the cup and saucer on the table next to Riordan. "Cook made cinnamon scones, sir. Would you care for one? I know how you enjoy them."

"After I tackle this rasher of bacon, I will. Thank you, Martin." Popping a forkful of curried eggs in his mouth, he nodded to his father, Julian Wollstonecraft, Viscount Tensbridge, as he strode into the room. All the Wollstonecraft men were tall and dark-haired, save his Uncle Garrett, his father's thirty-two-year-old half-brother. At the age of forty-five, his father had threads of gray at his temples but was often mistaken for someone younger. His detached, distinguished air bespoke of their venerated lineage.

"Already tucking in, I see." His father gave him an amused smile as he took his seat, content to allow Martin to serve him.

"I'm blasted hungry this morning. Perhaps it is the change in temperature," Riordan said between bites.

"Coffee this morning, my lord?" Martin asked.

"Yes. Coffee it is. And ham instead of bacon." Julian snapped open the linen napkin and laid it on his lap. "Riordan, where is your older brother?"

Older by fifteen minutes, Aidan was the heir apparent, and Riordan was fine with it. His paternal twin had stumbled in at three in the morning; he couldn't help but hear his brother cursing and bumping into furniture across the hall. "Still asleep, I believe."

His father sighed. "Martin, send one of the footmen to rouse my slugabed son."

"At once, my lord." The butler inclined his head toward one of the footmen, who exited the dining area.

Garrett walked into the room dressed as if he had come straight from the barn, which he had, seeing he spent all his time with horses. His uncle had inherited his red hair, pale skin, and freckles from his Scottish mother. Close to six and a half feet in height, his barrel chest and massive shoulders were a stark contrast to the leaner musculature of the rest of the men. Much like a medieval Highlander, Riordan mused.

"Before you ask, brother, I wiped my muddy boots," Garrett said as he moved to the sideboard. His uncle managed to pile more food on his plate than Riordan had. Sitting across the table, Garrett immediately started to eat as the footmen brought toast and poured his tea.

"How's Starlight doing?" Julian asked while cutting his ham into meticulous bite-sized pieces.

"She hasn't foaled yet," Garrett replied. "Going to be a long siege, I imagine. The stable lads are watching and will inform me of any developments."

Aidan entered the room with a short, unsteady gait, looking the worse for wear. He plopped down next to Garrett. "Coffee, Martin, and lots of it. Bring me nothing else, or I shall puke, for certain."

Julian curled his lip in obvious distaste. "Out gambling and whoring again? Best not let your grandfather see the state of you. Sit up straight." Aidan sneered but did as he was told. "Martin, bring the heir toast and cheese. You will eat and get that insolent expression off your face. Look at the state of you, unkempt, eyes bloodshot. We will be speaking about this at great length after the meeting concludes."

Riordan did not envy his brother.

He's in the soup now.

But when had he not been with their father? It was as if Aidan acted in such a way to rile him on purpose.

As always, Oliver Wollstonecraft entered last. Tall and regal, his grandfather defied Father Time, standing as straight and tall as his sons and grandsons. He was a sterling example of exemplary hereditary vim and vigor and amazingly good health. Riordan's great-grandfather, the old earl, passed away five years ago, and he'd remained a striking figure well into his eighties. Of all the maladies to cause death, it was a winter chill that took him.

"Ah, all here. Excellent." The earl took his seat at the head of the table while Martin and the footmen laid tea, coffee, and various food items in front of him—and Aidan, who turned a sickening shade of green at the sight of it. Riordan smirked. Having his brother cast up his accounts would certainly add drama to the gathering.

Attendance was mandatory at these family meetings. The earl would brook no argument or accept any excuses for not being present. What was discussed at these compulsory summits? Ways to further the family's progressive agenda.

Though distantly related to Mary Wollstonecraft, the late-eighteenth-century scholar, philosopher, and advocate of women's rights, and to her daughter, Mary Wollstonecraft Shelley, essayist and the novelist of the gothic tale Frankenstein, the men of Wollstonecraft Hall were no less involved in liberal causes.

When he finished serving, Martin sat next to the earl, pen, ink, and parchment at the ready to record the minutes. The footmen moved efficiently around the table, bringing the scones, cheese turnovers, and fruit and refilling beverages as the men conversed.

"I've received word that our eccentric neighbor, Sir Walter Keenan, has passed away," the earl stated.

Riordan's mouth quirked with amusement. Not at the news of Sir Walter's death but at the fact that his grandfather found him eccentric, considering what society thought of the Wollstonecrafts. Sir Walter was an ex-soldier, granted a knighthood for his bravery in the Peninsular War at Salamanca in 1808. Since returning home from the army in 1819, he had lived as a hermit.

"Since he is unmarried, the property is passing to his next of kin," his grandfather continued. "His niece, a widow, I don't know her name, is the beneficiary. He's been our neighbor for more than thirty-five years. Someone should put in an appearance at his funeral."

Julian shook his head. "The widow will be inheriting a run-down manor, to say the least. I will not be able to attend. I am heading to London, the autumn session of parliament, as I've meetings with Lord Ashley." Since his father had a courtesy title, he didn't sit in the House of Lords. He served as a member of parliament for this region of Kent, though he often worked with the upper chamber on many bills.

Riordan would not be able to attend the funeral either, but he decided he would leave his announcement for the end of the gathering. Why stir up the hornet's nest at this juncture?

"How go the discussions for restricting the number of work hours?" Garrett asked as he sipped his tea. All the other men gave him incredulous looks. "What? I read the papers, and I am a member of this family. I have broadminded views."

"I'm working with Lord Ashley to reduce the workweek to sixty hours for women and children," Julian replied. "We are being fought tooth and nail. I predict a compromise somewhere between sixty and seventy."

The earl harrumphed. "Still too long."

Julian buttered his cinnamon scone. "I agree, but most peers strongly believe women and children are an integral part of a family's earning power, and under the man of the house's command. Most do not want any regulations at all."

Riordan glanced across the table at his brother. Aidan's expression held a combination of nausea and boredom. "I've read that one out of every three citizens is under the age of fifteen, which is the reason many children labor in textile mills and coal mines," Riordan said.

Julian nodded. "True. There should be regulations in place to protect the innocent. Another touchy subject is repealing the Corn Laws."

"Blasted protectionism. I was against it from the first," the earl boomed. "By imposing restrictions on imported wheat, which in turn inflates grain prices, all it has done is managed to further deepen and expand the wretched poverty infecting this country."

"I agree, Father. It is going to be a nasty fight. I predict it will shake the foundations of the British government." Julian popped a piece of scone into his mouth and swallowed. "You should go with me to London instead of waiting until the middle of next month. There are many battles to be fought, and we need every progressive voice we can muster."

"Yes, perhaps I will," the earl replied.

Riordan's heart swelled with pride as he listened to his father's impassioned words.

The subject changed to the running of the estate, and Garrett brought everyone up to date on the horse breeding, farming, and the surrounding tenants.

Aidan remained silent, slowly picking away at his toast and cheese.

"Aidan," Julian said, his voice tight with annoyance. "You are the heir. You will be carrying our progressive torch into the future. Have you nothing to offer?"

Aidan looked up, a bored expression on his face. "Not this morning, Father."

The rumblings of a heated argument simmered near the surface, and because of it, Riordan decided to make his announcement to divert away from a family spat. At least, he hoped it would. "I have news. I have accepted a position as schoolmaster in the town of Carrbury, in East Sussex."

The table grew quiet, and all eyes turned to him. Well, he'd shocked them into silence. Might as well continue. "One of our main concerns is neglected, exploited, and abused children. Trying to pass compulsory education is defeated at every turn for the exact reason you mentioned, Father. The notion that children be kept uneducated and ignorant so that it makes them better workers is inherently heinous."

The men all grumbled, nodding, and agreeing with his assessment. Even Aidan reacted with a brisk nod. Riordan pushed on. "Education reform is achingly slow. We all know it will take decades of small, incremental changes before education for all becomes enforced. But changes are being made. The Ragged School Union was set up this past spring. Schools are opening all across Great Britain, not only charity schools. There's a new concept: board schools."

He had their complete attention. Even the butler listened in. "Fee-paying schools have been around for centuries but are only available to those in the upper class who can afford them. Board schools would charge landowners and businesses a small fee to be administered by an elected board of local officials. One of these schools has been set up in Carrbury. I applied for the position of schoolmaster, was interviewed, and was accepted. I did not go by Wollstonecraft. I applied as Mr. Riordan Black." Black was his middle name, his mother's surname. "One of the board members knows my true identity, as I had to prove my education credentials, but he agreed to keep it secret so that it would not draw too much attention to the school. I will be able to gather information, implement my reforms, and observe if they take root."

"I am exceedingly proud of you, Son," Julian said, the words spoken warmly. A derisive snort came from Aidan, but their father ignored it.

"As am I, Riordan. All the information you gather will only strengthen our cause. How far away is Carrbury?" his grandfather asked.

"About twenty-two miles south of here, less than a day's ride. I'm to report there in five days' time. The small township and surrounding area cover a population of about seven hundred, and I'm told I may have upward of thirty-five children of various ages in the classroom."

"Shrewd of you to conceal the name. Come and walk with me, Riordan, and we will discuss this development further. If there is no other business?" He glanced around the table. "I adjourn the meeting," the earl stated.

Aidan stood, but Julian shot him a thunderous look. "Sit. We have much to talk about."

"On that ominous note, I will return to the horses." Garrett took one last sip of tea, wiped his mouth, and stood. He strode over to Riordan and the earl, clasping Riordan on the shoulder. "Well done. You do this family proud."

He was genuinely touched and not used to such gracious words from his self-contained uncle. With a nod, Garrett left the room.